THE
Christmas
VISITOR

THE
Christmas
VISITOR

AN AMISH ROMANCE

LINDA BYLER

Good Books

New York, New York

THE CHRISTMAS VISITOR

Copyright © 2018 by Linda Byler

All rights reserved. No part of this book may be reproduced in any manner without the express written consent of the publisher, except in the case of brief excerpts in critical reviews or articles. All inquiries should be addressed to Good Books, 307 West 36th Street, 11th Floor, New York, NY 10018.

Good Books books may be purchased in bulk at special discounts for sales promotion, corporate gifts, fund-raising, or educational purposes. Special editions can also be created to specifications. For details, contact the Special Sales Department, Good Books, 307 West 36th Street, 11th Floor, New York, NY 10018 or info@skyhorsepublishing.com.

Good Books is an imprint of Skyhorse Publishing, Inc.®, a Delaware corporation.

Visit our website at www.goodbooks.com.

10 9 8 7 6 5 4 3 2 1

Library of Congress Cataloging-in-Publication Data is available on file.

ISBN: 978-1-68099-376-9
eBook ISBN: 978-1-68099-093-5

Cover design by Koechel Peterson & Associates, Inc., Minneapolis, Minnesota

Printed in Canada

Table of Contents

Chapter One

I<small>T WAS THE ROCKING CHAIR'S SQUEAK THAT</small> started the tears. The high, annoying chirp would have driven him to find the WD-40, turn the rocker upside down, and liberally spray the irritating spot, satisfied only when it was completely silenced.

She could smell the WD-40. She could see him kneeling there—his dark eyebrows drawn down in concentration, his eyes flat, the perfect nose beneath them, his wide mouth unsmiling, but only for a short time. He was known to talk a lot and smile as much, his hands moving, alive, so animated, so interesting.

She didn't realize right away that her tears were falling on little Benjamin. They dampened the downy hair of the five-week-old son she was holding, darkening and flattening it in sections. Clucking and crooning, she moved a thin finger delicately across the wet spots, trying not to wake him, and then bent her head to kiss the warm, rounded cheek.

Here in her arms lay Ben's final gift to her, born three months after Ben had fallen at the barn raising at Elam Glick's down along 896 near Christiana. Ruth never had a chance to say goodbye.

Life went on, she found. It moved right along, whether she decided to go with it or not. It was impossible to speak of her grief and express it properly when it was a twisting, tumbling void that threatened to swallow her up the minute she didn't move along with life. Her children were the motivation that got her up and moving after she'd been chewed up and spit out after the viewing and the funeral.

The rain that day had been so fitting. The weeping pines bent their fragrant green boughs to allow the fresh April showers to drip from one branch to the next below. The black umbrellas sprouted like grieving mushrooms with the black-clad members of the Old Order Amish huddled beneath them.

Rows of horses and buggies were tied along the well-kept white painted fence. Numbers had been chalked in white on the sides of the gray buggies. Ruth had ridden in the buggy marked with a simple 1. The first buggy. His wife and children following the coffin, a plain wooden box laid reverently in the horse drawn hearse.

Back at the farm, where the services had been held in the shop, the women had packed sandwiches of Lebanon bologna and white American cheese with mayonnaise on wheat bread. It was a token of *sark feltich* (caring) hearts, as was the custom, a snack to tide them over after the long services and a boost of nutrition for the children before the burial.

She couldn't keep him, although she'd tried, touching that lifeless face just once more. In the end, as the minister's voice droned on in a sing-song cadence and the pines wept, they had closed the coffin and lowered it, and the granules of Lancaster County soil hit the wood with a sound that was now a permanent part of her.

The smell of wet soil would always remind her of that day. So would Lebanon bologna.

"Mam!"

The call pulled her abruptly back to reality. Struggling, she tried to get out of the chair and then answered, "Lillian, *ich komm*! (I come!)"

Tenderly Ruth settled little Benjamin, pulling the soft baby blanket up to his waist, no farther, for in August the nights were warm. She moved swiftly down the short hallway into her bedroom where Lillian, the rowdy three year old, sat straight as a small tree trunk, saying she was thirsty. She wanted chocolate milk, but Ruth said, no, no chocolate milk, just water. Even when Lillian kicked off the covers and threw a fit, she remained firm, gave her a cold drink of water, and promised chocolate milk in the morning.

She checked on the older girls. Barbara was on her side, her shoulders rising and falling beneath the thin, handed down nightgown, the one Esther had worn for many summers.

She listened at the door of the boys' room, but all was quiet and peaceful, the darkness a comfort somehow. Roy was nine and Elmer ten. They were lively young boys with energy to spare, now that they'd been transplanted to the small rancher with vinyl siding on Hoosier Road.

She couldn't have kept the farm, with the depressing economy, so they said. A recession. Land prices had fallen—were falling. So she'd sold out to the highest bidder. The amount fell short of the accumulated debt. As was the custom, the people stood by her with donations, alms, and benefit suppers. It had all amounted to an amazing sum.

Levi King had provided the house. She had no income, other than her quilting. There was nothing else she could do, with six children to care for. If she did get a job, which she would need to do—and soon—she would simply need to hire a babysitter, the way the English people did. She didn't have much choice.

The church "kept" their widows as did kind relatives. Her parents, his parents—they all gave and *sarked* (cared for) Ben *sei* Ruth (his wife, Ruth). But she could not go on sponging off of others forever.

She showered and shampooed her thick brown hair, donned a thin nightgown, and pulled a hairbrush through her heavy, wet tresses.

Ruth Miller was only thirty years old—small, petite, and much too young in appearance for her thirty years. She leaned over the bathroom sink to fasten the snaps of her cotton robe, pulled back her hair, and went outside to sit on the porch to allow her hair to dry, if only for a moment.

The crickets were noisy, and the katydids noisier still, shrieking their plaintive cries from the locust tree by the shed. The sky was alive with twinkling stars, but the leaves of the old oak tree hung limp in the hot August night with hardly a breeze to stir them. Somewhere a lonesome dog howled, starting up a series of sharp yipping from a neighboring one.

Ruth lifted her face as she loosened her hair and ran her fingers through it to help dry faster.

Well, Ben, it's been a long day. I think little Benjamin will be very much like you. Active, alert, quick to speak. Lillian just drives me crazy. I never was good with her. I can't start pitying myself now, but you were so perfect for her. I think that is part of her problem.

Elmer had a bad day. He helped Priscilla pull corn for the roadside stand, and she wouldn't allow him to sell any—just sent him home with five dollars for three hours of work. Is that fair?

Ben, how am I going to make it? Coal is up to two hundred and some dollars a ton. I could burn wood, but is it really much cheaper? I can't afford propane.

Esther needs to have her eyes examined, I feel sure, but there is no extra money. I'm too proud to beg. And I'm afraid I'm not very good with the money I do have. I bought two rugs at Walmart, along with my groceries, and now I feel I shouldn't have.

What about Esther's eyes?

Ruth watched the stars, as if one might answer, then closed her eyes and prayed to the One far above the stars, the Presence in whom she placed her faith from day to day.

"*Unser Vater in dem Himmel* (Our Father who art in Heaven)," she murmured.

Later, she fell asleep the minute her head touched the pillow. She slept dreamlessly until Benjamin became restless and woke her with his soft little grunts, turning his head from side to side as the hunger in his little belly disturbed him.

Ruth sighed, knowing it would do no good to try the pacifier. She rolled out of bed, gathered him up, and cuddled him beside her.

The sun soon emerged above the horizon, and she knew the pulsing orange ball of heat would send the mercury on the old plastic thermometer up to well past 90 degrees.

She was up and dressed by six o'clock, wearing a blue, short-sleeved summer dress with a black bib apron tied over it and her washed and well worn white organdy covering pinned neatly on her head.

It was always good to get an early start. Quietly, her bare feet whispering across the floor, she picked up the plastic Rubbermaid hamper from the corner of the bathroom. She grabbed the dripping washcloth she saw dangling from the side of the white bathtub and threw it on top. She carried her load to the laundry room, where the Maytag wringer washer stood solidly attached to the floor, the plastic rinse tubs beside it.

As quietly as possible, she opened and closed the screen door, then hurried to the diesel shanty attached to the barn. There she flipped a switch, turned the key, and was rewarded by the grinding sound of the Lister diesel engine coming to life.

Blue smoke puffed from the gray exhaust pipe, staining the cement blocks around it with a black ring as usual. She closed the diesel shanty door and hurried back to the house.

There was always pressure on wash day to hurry and finish before the little ones awoke. She should be okay today—Benjamin's last feeding had been at four thirty—if Lillian stayed quiet.

Water gushed out of the hose with a turn of the spigot, filling the large washer. She added a cup of Tide with Bleach and opened the handle on the air line, allowing the compressed air from the tank behind the diesel shanty to power the air motor beneath the wringer washer with a rhythmic movement.

Quickly, she separated the laundry. Whites went in first. She closed the spigot after the rinse tub was full and added a capful of Downy, then went to put the teakettle on for her coffee.

She could already feel beads of sweat forming on her upper lip and glanced at the thermometer. She resigned herself to the heat but sighed when she heard Lillian's grumpy howls from the bedroom. Tying on the apron filled with clothespins,

Ruth scuttled back the hallway saying, "Shh!"

Lillian was not happy. Her eyes were heavy with drowsiness from waking up before she was really finished sleeping, and she was every bit as ill-tempered as usual. Ruth swept her up, wrapped her arms around the small form of her daughter, and held her tightly, raining teasing little kisses on her sticky face.

Lillian fought, turning her head and grimacing, her pigtails stuck out in every direction, her muffled laughter emerging.

"*Do net!* (Don't!)"

"My funny girl! You're going on the couch!"

Dumping her unceremoniously on the blue sofa, Ruth pulled the lavender nightgown over Lillian's bent knees and pressed down on her legs, making her bounce slightly.

"*Do net!*"

But she was giggling, her round face wreathed in smiles, her blue eyes creased at the corners, and Ruth smiled back.

"I want chocolate milk!"

How could one mighty little three year old remember, through eight hours of sleep, that she had wanted that chocolate milk the night before and was refused?

She never gave up, often being "chastened" for outright disobedience. If she was told repeatedly not to get into the pea patch, that was exactly where she was fifteen minutes later, like a little rabbit, hunkered down and eating peas as fast as she could, her blue eyes completely innocent.

Ruth would not allow the despair to penetrate her sense of well-being. She pushed back the sinking feeling of being completely incapable of handling her six children, her life. It was one day, one hour at a time.

If Lillian had been promised chocolate milk the evening before, that is what she would have. Ruth stirred Hershey's syrup into the cold milk in the Sippy cup and took it to Lillian, who smiled widely, without remembering to say thank you.

Ruth hung the whites on the wheel line, pushing the clothes out over the back yard after pinning them securely with wooden clothespins from the apron around her waist.

The air was still and already humid. She heard the purring of the diesel back on the farm, the rhythmic clip clopping sound of an approaching team, robins scolding from the electric wire beside the road.

She'd mow the grass today after she finished her cleaning. It was Friday, the day she usually accomplished all three major tasks of cleaning, laundry, and yard work. The boys would pull weeds in the garden and push the hand cultivator through it.

The door opened only a sliver, and bright blue eyes peeked out. The door was pushed open wider, and a tousled head appeared, followed by "Hi, Mam!"

"Well, good morning, Barbara!"

"Are you good?"

"Yes, I'm very good."

"Did you sleep good?"

"Oh, yes!"

Barbara came over and laid her head against Ruth's waist as her arms went around her mother. Ruth held her close, a wet washcloth clutched in her hand. She inhaled the sun and dirt and not quite properly rinsed hair.

"Mmm, Barbara. *Ich gleich dich so arich* (I love you so much)."

Barbara was the one endowed with a caring spirit, loving and gentle and kind to all, except for Roy. Roy was the one single irritant of her life, the fly in her chicken corn soup, the rain on her parade, the fingernail across her blackboard.

"Esther's awake."

"Good. Is she with Lillian?"

"Yes. Lillian wants Trix."

"Did she get her some?"

"They're all gone."

"Would you please check on the baby?"

Barbara left immediately, and Ruth shook her head, always appreciative of her five year old's willingness to obey.

They ate dippy eggs, stewed saltine crackers,

and buttered toast for their breakfast as they sat gathered around the kitchen table near the sunny east windows. The windows sat low in the wall, allowing all that morning light to enter.

The table was a solid oak extension one, made by Noah Fisher down below Atglen before Ben and Ruth were married. The chairs were wheat chairs, the spindles on the back splayed out so that they resembled sheaves of wheat, all made of solid oak.

The tablecloth on the table was a durable double-knit fabric from Lizzie Zook's Dry Goods Store in Intercourse. Ruth had hemmed it herself, and it was a fine red and white gingham, service-able for years, as long as she used her dependable Shout spray on the grease spots before immersing it in the hot water in the wringer washer.

Ruth's dishes were Corelle, the set her sisters had given her on the day she became Ben's bride. She still had most of them after eleven years, which was remarkable considering what they'd been through.

The kitchen cabinets were oak as well, fairly new, with the gas refrigerator set neatly in the space created for it. A healthy green fern sprouted from a brown pot suspended above the sink by a macramé holder, and the canister set was brown ironstone to match. By the low windows, there were more potted plants—a fig tree, another fern, and a few African violets.

The hutch against the west wall was made by Noah Fisher as well and contained the china that Ben had given her a few weeks before the wedding. He'd been so humble, almost shy.

Ruth loved pretty things, her artistic touch showing in her ability to maintain a nice home, although it was all done in simplicity, with common sense, the way the Amish *ordnung* (rules) required.

She felt blessed, having this small single story house and being able to live in it without paying rent. Levi King simply refused it, and Lizzie told her in whispered tones they wouldn't feel right taking her money, then closed her eyes and kept them closed for so long that Ruth had a terrible urge to laugh. Then she felt like crying and wringing this dear, plump woman's hand, but she just gave up and hugged her. Without the support of the Amish community, she'd never make it—that was one sure thing.

Her family's support was tremendous, her bank account still containing the last of their generosity. Her emotional support was bolstered frequently by caring relatives and was as essential as the air she breathed. But some things can only be spoken in solitude, things other people need not know.

Chapter Two

ELMER AND ROY DID A GOOD JOB IN THE garden, for all of thirty minutes, before they gasped and staggered toward the old oak tree, flopped down on their backs, and flung their arms across their foreheads—each movement seemingly synchronized, like swimmers.

"Mam!"

The howl was in unison, too.

Ruth stopped pushing the reel mower and wiped the perspiration from her forehead as the blood pounded in her ears. She answered with a calm, "Yes, boys."

"It's too hot! It's cruel to make us work in the garden."

"Oh, come on! You're men. You're tough!"

Elmer's head flopped back and forth as if it hadn't been properly attached.

"It's 100 degrees," Roy wailed, his despair bringing a deep mirth from someplace Ruth had almost forgotten.

It would soon be five months since Ben had fallen, leaving her to journey alone. She had never thought she would laugh ever again, certainly not within five years. But life kept on going. And it was the children that mattered. They gave her reason to go on living. And here was Roy, making her laugh, deeply and sincerely.

Flopping down to sit beside them, she bowed her head and gave in to her laughter, squeezing her eyes shut, lifting her face, and howling with it. She didn't cry hysterically at the end either.

Roy and Elmer looked at their mother, then both sat up and watched her with serious concern.

"Oh my!" Ruth gasped, wiping her eyes. "Sorry, I wasn't *schputting* (mocking) you."

Roy eyed her warily.

"Yes, you were."

"Nah-uh!"

"What else was it?"

"I guess it just struck me funny, because I'm hot and miserable, too. It is too warm. But I'm almost finished. We'll come back out this evening, and you can finish the garden while I run the weed eater."

Elmer looked as if he couldn't believe his good luck.

"Can we go swimming?"

Ruth considered his question.

"Would it be possible to pick the green beans and take them to Mrs. Beadle first?"

"I think so."

Completely rejuvenated, they bent their backs to the task with the plastic buckets by their sides. The sun suddenly seemed much more comfortable than it had ten minutes before.

Esther was in the house filling her usual role as the bossy older sister. She had her little bib apron tied around her waist and was caring for Benjamin while scolding Lillian for getting beads in the baby's face.

"Lillian, now get away from him!" she screeched, her dark hair wet with the sweat from her forehead, her dark blue eyes intense, her hands on her hips, for all the world a replica of a little biddy hen protecting her chicks.

Ruth washed her hands at the sink and dried them on her apron.

"Your face is red!" Lillian shouted.

"It's hot outside," Ruth answered, smiling.

"Mam, you have to stay in here. That Lillian is a mess. She won't listen to me. She just keeps getting at Baby Benjamin. She's driving me nuts!"

"Now, Esther. Don't say it like that. That's going a bit overboard."

"Well, I don't know how to say it so that you'll listen."

Ruth hid a smile as she stooped to pick up

Lillian, buckling down yet again to the responsibility of raising this brood of six children alone without ever showing the worries that threatened to overtake her.

When Ben was alive, they had been busy. The farm required physical labor day after day, but the responsibilities and the decision making had been shared. It made a difference. There was so much to be shouldered alone.

The first thing to go had been the battery lamps. It was easier to fill a plastic can with kerosene to fill the lamps they used in the bathroom and bedroom than it was lug those heavy twelve-volt batteries around. Yes, the kerosene was smelly, and she had to wash the glass lamp chimneys each week, but it was easier to manage. She had also learned to change the propane tank for the kitchen lamp, a job she had never accomplished before Ben died.

Now she also had to harness Pete, the driving horse, all by herself, and with Elmer lifting the shafts, hitch him to the buggy to drive to church or the grocery store herself. She had become used to it, and it wasn't so bad, though she did often worry about driving alone with the children.

The responsibility of making decisions about the children was not easy, ever. Should Elmer be forced to return to Priscilla's corn patch? Would it be best to make him continue to work hard at a job he despised? Or should she take pity on him and allow him to stop? Which was best—building character or understanding his total dislike of Priscilla and her weedy corn patch? That was when she needed Ben so badly. That was when she felt defeated, but only as much as she allowed herself, she soon learned.

All her life, courage had just been a word—much like virtue or hope or fear or any other word—until she'd been alone. Courage was now a noun. She had to buckle it on, like a harness or a back pack, click the plastic fasteners into place, take a deep breath, and just get going with it.

Dealing with Esther and Lillian took courage. Dealing with perfect little Barbara and her abrasive, yet sensitive, brother took courage as well. And on and on.

But this day ended with a perfect late summer evening, and as the sun slid behind the cornfields and the twilight folded itself softly down around them, they took a pitcher of iced mint tea out on the front porch and a bag of Tom Sturgis pretzels with some ranch dressing to dip them in. The lawn was clipped evenly, the edges of the flower beds were trimmed, and the garden contained no weeds—at least as far as Ruth could tell from the porch. Benjamin was settled for the night, and Lillian curled up on her lap, her tousled little head quiet at last. And Ruth knew she was not alone. God was right there with her and the children, supplying backpacks full of courage when she needed it.

The Lord giveth, and the Lord taketh away. Yes, of course. It was God's will to take Ben, for reasons we don't know, her mother had said. So had Aunt Lydia and Eva. The true test of faith is in accepting and trusting God when life's events leave us without understanding.

Why her? Ruth had questioned many times in her heart, but only once to her mother.

Dear Mam. Ruth's rock of comfort. When all else failed, her Mam was there with her large blue eyes and wrinkles and crow's feet that all somehow reflected her life—the garden, the wringer washer, the harrowing, hay making, cooking and baking, laughing and crying, teaching, and being stern in the way only Mam could, living her life with Dat, her life's partner for more than thirty-five years.

Tomorrow, Mam would come for the day, bringing a spring wagon loaded with corn. Incredible, her specialty.

"Did you know Mommy (Grandmother) is coming tomorrow?" Ruth asked the children.

"Is she?"

"Yes, we'll be freezing corn."

"Goody!" Esther clapped her hands.

"Can we eat all we want all day long?'

"Of course!"

The prospect of having Mommy Lapp come

to their house the next day provided a sense of anticipation. Their happiness replaced the usual melancholy that often settled over them at night, when the children missed Ben most.

Mommy Lapp might let the boys drive Ginger, her trustworthy driving horse, if they needed something at the store. Ruth glanced at Elmer, knowing what he was thinking, and grinned.

"You might be allowed to drive Ginger."

Elmer laughed, then watched his mother's face before saying, "Mam, I worry about training a horse. Who will buy me a buggy, or teach me to drive my own horse if…Dat is…." He stopped and swallowed, then reached self consciously for another pretzel as if that act of normalcy could cover his embarrassment.

"Oh, that's a long way off, Elmer."

But after the children were in bed, Ruth returned to the porch. She aimlessly rocked in the wooden rocker and thought of what he'd said.

Who would? She didn't think about being married to someone else. How could she ever be unfaithful to the memory of Ben? He lived on in her heart and in her mind. It wouldn't be right.

She'd teach Elmer. Somehow they'd acquire the money for a horse and buggy. Elmer had always been a serious thinker, well beyond his years, and now, without Ben, he was especially so. They would manage.

No, she could not imagine subjecting these children to a new relationship. It would not be fair to them. It would be entirely different if she had only one or two children who were too young to understand. But at the age of ten, it would be too hard for Elmer and even the others—except perhaps her little Benjamin.

In the morning, the children were up and dressed, except for Lillian, who hadn't slept long enough the night before, when Ruth's mother drove up to the barn with the corn piled high on the back of the black spring wagon.

Ruth hurried out to help her unhitch, followed by the children, leaving little Benjamin howling in his bouncy seat.

"*Ach* (Oh) my!"

Ruth hurried back into the house, crooning as she took up the unhappy newborn and cuddled him against her shoulder, bouncing him and patting his back. She looked out at her mother, surrounded by the children, her back bent slightly, her gray apron lifted to one side as she reached into the oversized pocket sewn on the side of her dress and extracted a heaping handful of Tootsie Rolls—every flavor imaginable.

Ruth smiled, knowing the sugar-laden candy would just have to be consumed before breakfast as Mommy Lapp pooh-poohed the idea that candy wasn't healthy. Ruth figured scrambled eggs and toast could aid its digestion.

Her mother entered the kitchen. She was a small woman with a rounded stomach and a bit of fullness around the hips, having borne eleven children of her own. She said she needed the extra padding. It was what kept her going. Her hair was pure white, neatly rolled at the sides, and pinned in the back beneath her large, white covering.

Mam was a *dienna's frau* (minister's wife). Her coverings were large, and she wore a belt apron pinned around her waist. Her clothes were conservative as a good example for the younger generation. Radiating kindness and caring, her work-worn hands were always ready to be laid on a suffering one's shoulder or slipped about the waist with whispered words of condolence that were always as available as the air she breathed.

Mam sat down. She gathered Barbara in one arm and Esther in the other, stroking their backs and saying, "Oh, girls, it's so good to see you again. It's been too long. I make myself too busy in the summertime, *gel* (right), Ruth?"

"Well, no Mam, you still have Emma and Lydiann at home, plus all those big boys who should be dating and getting married. I declare they are spoiled with you for their mother."

Highest praise, Ruth knew, and she was rewarded by a smile of pure benediction.

"Oh."

That was all she said, but Ruth knew her mam

loved having her boys around her, cooking huge breakfasts for them with fried mush and dried beef gravy and applesauce and shoofly pie and hot chocolate.

"Couldn't Emma come?"

"No, she goes to market with Lydiann on Saturdays now, too."

"Really?"

"Yes, David Kind gave her a job at the produce stand."

"Well, that's good."

"Yes, she'll be glad for some spending money. Lydiann was so busy she could hardly keep up with the customers, so she said something to David about it, and he said Emma could start last week."

"Is that market so busy already?"

"Well, in New Jersey fresh produce from Lancaster is quite popular."

Ruth nodded.

Farmer's markets were a way of life for many single Amish girls who worked long hours on the weekends selling produce, baked goods, meats and cheeses, or prepared foods like chicken, pulled pork, and a variety of barbeque. They were huge, indoor markets with many different vendors, bustling places filled with homemade or homegrown food, mostly within a 100-mile radius of the Amish farms of Lancaster County.

There was a high-pitched shriek from Ruth's room, and dutiful Barbara went to find Lillian, reappearing with the crying three year old on one hip. Lillian was indignantly wailing and hitting her sister.

"Lillian, *do net*!" Ruth called from her rocking chair where she was feeding Benjamin.

Instantly, Ruth's mam was on her feet, trying to take Barbara's heavy, writhing load from her and saying, "*Komm*, Lillian. *Komm. Mommy iss do* (Grandmother is here)."

Lillian's shrieks only increased in volume, so Barbara let her slide to the kitchen floor, where she resumed her howling. When Mommy tried to pick her up, Lillian twisted and turned, her legs

flailing, her nightgown revealing the large dispos-
able diaper she still wore.

"*Ich vill my tootie!* (I want my pacifier!)"

Quickly, Barbara scuttled down the hallway to
look for the missing pacifier, which, when present-
ed, was refused. The shrieking resumed. Without
a word, Ruth rose from the rocking chair, handed
the baby to her mother, and bent to pick up her
struggling daughter. She took her directly to the
laundry room, where she administered a firm
"reprimand," letting Lillian understand that such
behavior was completely unacceptable by using
the age-old method of the Plain people, who still
honored the meaning of molding a young child's
will.

Later, with Lillian's head on her shoulder and
her pacifier in her mouth, Ruth explained to her
that throwing a fit was not allowed as she was a
big girl now. Lillian hiccupped and sniffed but
stayed quiet, watching her grandmother warily.

Mommy cooked a large pan of scrambled eggs
and filled the broiler of the gas stove with slices of

homemade bread. She sadly noted the absence of bacon or sausage in Ruth's refrigerator that contained so little, but she said nothing.

"I brought a coffee cake. Elmer, can you go get it? It's under the seat."

"I'll go!" Roy yelled, almost upsetting his chair in his urgency to please his grandmother.

Later the women drank coffee alone as the children unloaded the corn outside. Mam asked Ruth how she was managing, her large, blue eyes round pools of love and caring, which always and without fail produced tears she did not want to show.

Ruth nodded, struggling for control. She got up and grabbed a handful of Kleenex as she drew her upper lip down to help stay the onset of emotion.

"Alright," she said.

No, Mam, actually I am not doing well. I'm afraid I'm not doing the right thing with Lillian. I'm weak and tired, and I miss Ben so much I want to die sometimes. I'm afraid my money will soon be all gone, and I feel guilty for everything I spend because it's really someone else's hard-earned money.

But she did not say that.

"Just alright?"

Ruth nodded, unable to speak. She was afraid one word would strangle her and open the flood-gates of self-pity and grief and helplessness and inadequacy.

Mam cut a slice of coffee cake with the side of her fork, put it carefully in her mouth, and chewed, wisely allowing Ruth time to salvage her pride.

"It's Lillian, isn't it?'

Ruth nodded, avoiding her mother's eyes. Down came those mother's hands, the hands of a *dienna's frau* like the hands of an angel, taking up both of Ruth's and accompanied by healing words of praise and encouragement.

"Ruth, you did exactly the right thing. You amaze me with the quiet way you have with these children. Lillian is different, but you know as well as I do that not one child is the same as the others. They are all given a different nature, and Lillian is just…well."

Ruth lifted her eyes to her mother's, saw the humor, those little stars of goodwill, and laughed.

"Mam, you know what she said the other day? She said she is going to put Benjamin in the rabbit hutch where he belongs."

Mam laughed heartily.

"I know, Ruth. She's a character. She's jealous, likely, of the new baby. And on top of that, she doesn't really understand about Ben."

"You noticed the Pamper?"

"Yes."

"She's three, Mam. I've never had a problem training any of my children. Till now. She's so stubborn. She knows better, but she just doesn't care. It simply tries me to the limit."

"And she will often continue to do so— throughout her life, no doubt. She reminds me so much of your sister, Betty."

"Help us all!" Ruth said, laughing.

Betty was Ruth's sister, who had taught school for many years. She often spoke her mind to distraught parents, roiling the calm waters around her with blunt remarks that were not always well received. She had finally married a bachelor at the age of twenty-seven, and her marriage was less than peaceful now, even after only a year and a half together.

"Poor Reuben."

"Oh, he takes care of himself."

And so the conversation carried on throughout the day as only the chatter of mothers and daughters can. They hopped from one subject to another as they sat on folding lawn chairs under the oak tree in the backyard with wheelbarrow loads of corn and piles of husks surrounding them. The dishpans were piled high with the heavy ears of yellow corn, brushed clean with vegetable brushes.

The two-burner outdoor propane cooker bubbled away as it cooked the corn, which, after being heated through, was plunged into the cold water in the cooling tubs. Roy manned the tubs, and the cold water from the hose often strayed, spraying his sisters or Elmer.

When the corn was completely cooled, the dishpans were filled again and set on a bench where Mam and Ruth cut it from the cobs with sharp knives. Some of it was creamed by sliding the cooled ears of corn across the stainless steel corn creamer. The device had a long, rounded shaft with jagged teeth built into the center, which tore the kernels into small pieces and creamed it for baked corn or just to be eaten with butter and salt.

They set up the corn eating station on the wooden picnic table with salt and butter at each end and a Corelle platter of sliced tomatoes, a jar of mayonnaise, and a loaf of sliced whole wheat bread in the middle.

For a small woman, Mam could eat so many ears of corn that it was almost alarming. She applied the butter with a liberal rolling of the ear of corn, over and over across the cold goodness of it. She poured on the salt with the same generous hand and continued by lowering her head, her teeth crunching. She stopped only to roll her eyes and voice her pleasure before buttering another ear.

Ruth agreed. Corn, especially the variety called "Incredible," was exactly that—rows of perfect yellow kernels bursting with flavor and a sweetness so good it was impossible not to look for another good ear after finishing the first one.

They wiped away their perspiration and cooled themselves by drinking cold beverages and plunging their hands into the cold well water, which also helped tremendously.

"Lillian, *voss huscht* (What do you have)?" Mommy called.

Ruth shrieked and grabbed at the fat, green tomato worm Lillian was laying gently on top of the cooled ears of corn.

"My worm!" Lillian cried. She quickly picked it up and deposited it in the sandbox, where Ruth decided if she wanted to give the worm a ride with the plastic dump truck, she could.

And Mommy allowed Elmer to drive Ginger the whole way to the freezer, the electric one kept in an English neighbor's shed. Other Amish families also paid a set fee every month for the privilege of having a large chest freezer there.

Mommy told Elmer he was a good driver, even though he almost upset the spring wagon by turning too short. Later she sprouted a summer cold sore where she'd bitten down hard on her lip so she wouldn't yell in fright and perhaps hurt Elmer's feelings.

Chapter Three

AFTER THE DAY OF FREEZING CORN, RUTH also made spaghetti sauce, pizza sauce, salsa, and tomato soup, turning bucket after bucket of brilliant red sun-ripened tomatoes into row after row of colorful Ball jars of goodness, which were stored in the cold cellar with the pickles and red beets, the corn and zucchini relish. There was still applesauce to be done, and peaches and pears and grape jelly and grape juice.

School sewing, though, was on top of Ruth's list. It glared at her from beneath the square silver magnet on the refrigerator—the yellow slip of paper where she had written what she needed. Ten yards of Swedish knit, three yards of black apron material, shirts for the boys, buttons, black thread, sewing machine needles, hair pins.

School would start in a few weeks. The baby was crying from what seemed to be an angry case of heat rash that had developed overnight. Lillian had been stung by a carpenter bee—those wood borers that hovered around the barn's entrance like little bombers protecting their territory. Ruth was unsure if Lillian needed to see a doctor, the way her face was swollen and puffed up on one side so her eye had become a mere slit.

The heat had been unrelenting. It sapped Ruth's energy, so she often slept later than intended and then battled frustration, unable to accomplish all she wanted to.

Her steps were lighter now, coming in from the phone shanty, after having received a message from Aaron *sei* Hannah. Oh my. They were all coming on Thursday. The buddies. They were a precious group of women who had grown up with her. They had gone through their *rumspringa* (running around) years together and attended each other's weddings. They would bring their sewing machines! It was to be a covered dish gathering, and they would all bring something.

In the cool of the morning, Ruth slid onto the bench of the picnic table and folded her arms on the table. She lowered her head and cried just long enough to thank God for the gift of dear friends who were coming to pluck her out of discouragement.

Thursday arrived with the many teams turning into the driveway. They came bearing smiling faces, piles of little ones her own children's ages, casseroles, fruit, desserts, and salads. The women carried in their Berninas and Necchis and Singers and lugged along their twelve-volt batteries and inverters. The heavy blades from the Wiss scissors flashed as they cut into the fabric using the patterns Ruth kept in her folders in the bureau drawer.

The talking kept pace with the whirring of the

needles, humming along as pair after pair of black broadfall trousers appeared like magic, and the ten-yard roll of Swedish knit quickly disappeared.

Elmer and Roy each had a blue shirt and a red one. The ladies decided that wasn't enough, so they cut up the dusty green, too.

The buttons were sewn on, and the button-holes done by the machines. The women made quite a fuss about their mothers—or some of them—still making buttonholes by hand.

"Well, if you ask me, that is just dumb."

"My mother says it's her porch job. Sitting and relaxing in the evening."

"Seriously."

"*Unfashtendich* (senseless)."

"Why would you do that?"

There was talk of David Petersheim's new home being sold at auction.

"Four hundred and some thousand."

"That shop and all, no wonder."

"Who bought it?"

"Stop your sewing machines. Who?"

"A Mennonite?"

"Car Mennonite or Team?"

No one seemed to know. Somebody said the chap was English. Pretty old. They came to no conclusions.

Ruth wondered why Petersheims had sold out. It was a beautiful home set in the woods, all level land. She couldn't imagine living there. It looked so perfect.

"You're sure the last bidder wasn't Amish?"

"It's an Amish home."

And on and on.

They clucked over Lillian's face. Rachel said to put Swedish Bitters on it, without a doubt. Others were less sure with it being around the eye like that.

When they left, the new garments were all pressed and hung in the closets, but her whole house and lawn were a disaster.

No matter.

Ruth sang while she worked, sweeping, wiping Jello off walls, washing fingerprints from the windows, emptying trash cans. The boys picked up sandbox toys. Barbara and Esther hosed down the porch. Ruth got out the blue can of Raid and sprayed the walls around the doors, then slapped at flies inside the house and wiped them up with a tissue.

Later, they discovered the water trough in the barn contained more hay than water. It was soaked and slimy. Elmer voiced his opinion about buddies day, saying they all sat there and talked non-stop and let their children run wild.

But when school started, Ruth could send her three scholars down the road on their scooters, wearing the neon green, reflective vests she required. And she was thankful for her friends whose hearts had overflowed with love and kindness towards her and her family.

September brought cooler nights at least, but the heat persisted during the day. Her sister, Emma, helped her can peaches and pears. She made grape jelly after that, surveyed the stocked shelves in the cellar, and knew God was good.

Church services would be held at her parents' home the follow Sunday, in a *freme gegend* (a different district), so she ironed her Sunday covering with special care but was undecided about what to wear. Should it be her older black dress or one of the two newer ones she had made after Ben's death for her year of mourning? The older one was a bit too big around the waist, so she always felt as if her apron was falling off, no matter how tightly it was pinned.

She decided on the newer one that had a subtle swirl pattern in the material. The girls could wear their matching green dresses.

She laid out the boys' white shirts and their black vests and checked the trousers for any damage. One could never tell what might happen, the way boys played after services—especially at the homes of parents or relatives, when they stayed for the evening meal.

She buffed the boys' shoes, being careful to undo the black laces. Then she checked their drawers to make sure they had black socks, as she did not want them wearing white ones.

Her woven Sunday *kaevly* (basket) was packed carefully with Pampers on the bottom, an extra onesie, additional white socks, bottles, a pacifier, burp cloths, a small purse containing Goldfish and Cheerios, a keychain attached to a small plastic book, and three rolls of Smarties, enough to keep Lillian occupied at least for a short time.

Yes, she had her hands full with Esther, Barbara, and Lillian seated beside her and Benjamin, who was now two months old. But she learned it was possible to get through, with capable little Barbara as her helper. If only Lillian would cooperate, she'd be fine.

The morning was brisk and invigorating with the air bearing a hint of fall. The leaves were still green but hung tiredly, as if the summer's heat had made them weary and resigned to their coloring and final demise. The goldenrod was brilliant. The sumac had just begun to change color.

Pete was eager to go, so she let him run while half listening to Elmer's constant chatter as they passed homes, farms, and cornfields. He sat beside her, holding Benjamin, who was wide-eyed as the rumble of the steel wheels on the road made him aware of a change in his little world.

Ruth looked at him and smiled.

"*Voss? Bisht bye gay?* (What? Are you going away?)"

When a wide smile illuminated his face, Ruth bent sideways and kissed the top of his head.

"You're going to be good today, right?"

"You better watch where you're going."

"You want to drive?"

"Sure!"

"Give Benjamin to me."

So for the next few miles, Elmer was the attentive driver, carefully pulling on the right rein to keep Pete on his side of the road.

When they pulled into her parents' farm, there were already quite a few buggies parked in neat rows along the fence back by the corn crib and the implement shed.

"My goodness! No one going in the lane? I

hope we're not late."

"Nah," Elmer assured her, handing over the reins. He did not want to be responsible for the parking, which was sometimes a difficult thing to do with so many buggies already taking up a lot of the space. Of all the things that were changed by Ben's death, this one was one of the most difficult. Driving alone, a woman, so unaccustomed, having to worry about unhitching, even with Elmer's help. It was not exactly a humiliation. It was more the effort of staying calm and brave despite the appearance of being alone, different, the widow, the recipient of people's sympathy. She hated being alone in the buggy without Ben, always.

Where to go? Oh dear.

"Mam, over there," Elmer said, pointing a finger helpfully.

"All those boys," she said quietly.

"They won't look."

But they did. They all turned to watch as she pulled Pete up beside the silo and said, "Back!" as she tugged on the reins.

Pete had other ideas, of course—the cranky beast—so she was getting nowhere. Handing the reins to Elmer, she slid back the door of the buggy and was surprised to see one of the young men stepping out from the crowd and coming over to help her park.

Taking a firm grip on the horse's bit, he applied steady pressure, and Pete, who must have known he was in experienced hands, leaned back against the britchment and put the buggy right where Ruth had wanted it.

Then he stepped around to Ruth's side of the buggy. She stepped down from her seat in her black mourning dress and looked at him.

"*G'mya* (G'morning)."

"Hello."

"Shall I put your horse away?"

"You may, yes. Thank you."

There was a question in his eyes as plain as day, but he said nothing further. Ruth just went to the other side of the buggy and held out her arms for Benjamin as the young man reached under the seat for the halter and the neck rope. He went to release the buckle on Pete's bridle and looked at her, this small, young woman with all these children.

Ruth saw he had no beard, and his hat was well shaped, low in the back and pulled low over his eyes in the front. Someone had said at buddies day that Paul King's Anna was dating someone from the Dauphin County settlement. Oh, but it couldn't be him. Anna would be at her parents' church in a neighboring district.

Her helper was forgotten as Ruth was caught up in greeting relatives including some of her sisters she did not see on a regular basis. They had moved to neighboring counties and lived in smaller settlements of Amish folks.

Quite a fuss was made of little Benjamin's growth and his likeness to his father, though not without quick glances of kind sympathy and questioning her with their eyes.

Are you doing okay?

Did we say too much?

It's been nearly six months, hasn't it?

She shook hands with many friends and some women she did not know but who were all a part of the faith she was so accustomed to. By the time the first hymn was announced, Benjamin had had enough, and his wails became loud and urgent. Bending to tell Esther to remain seated, she made her way past her sisters, crossed the yard, and went into the house.

This was the home of her youth, the dear old stone house with the high ceilings and deep windowsills. Mam's wringer washer stood all by itself in the cement-floored laundry room with the drain in the floor beside it, like a milk house floor. Most younger women's washers were put in a closet or fastened to the floor, with drains underneath the washer and the rinse tubs and a lever to open or close them.

Not Mam. What would happen if there was a clog in there, she'd say, a hairpin or a safety pin? No sir. She let her water out of the wringer washer the old fashioned way—by unhooking the drain hose and letting it run across the floor and down the drain. Then, if there was an object in the washer that shouldn't be there, it came flying out in full view and could be picked up and thrown in the trash can.

Ruth smiled as she fed Benjamin, her eyes devouring the cabinets, the corner cupboard, the old extension table, the braided rug in front of the sink. The smells were identical to the ones of her youth with evidence of Mam's Shaklee products everywhere. The laundry soap, bath soap, dish detergent, window cleaner—all Shaklee.

The house was spotless, as usual, but then church services were here today, which had meant extra cleaning even if it wasn't entirely needed. The services were actually in the shop across the lawn, where Dat tinkered with woodworking or implement repair. It had been hosed down, the walls and windows washed, carpet laid, and benches set out. And now the services were beginning.

Rocking Benjamin, Ruth's head felt heavy, her

eyelids began to close, and she longed to take a nap. She had been awake at four that morning and was unable to get back to sleep with thoughts of driving Pete to her parents' house for church crowding out any possible slumber. Voices in the *kesslehaus* (wash house) brought her back from her slide into actual sleep.

"No, that's Jake's Sammie's Davey's boy. You know, *Huvvel* (planer) Dave, the one who has a woodworking shop somewhere up in Manheim."

"So is this guy the one who bought that property at the end of Hoosier Road?"

"I don't know."

"This guy's not bad looking. Why isn't he married?"

"Oh, he has a girlfriend. Paul's Anna."

"I see."

After Benjamin was satisfied, Ruth headed back to the shop, where she scooped up Lillian and held her close. She looked around at the congregation and saw Dat seated in the ministers' row, his gray hair and beard neat and clean, his head bent, likely sending up a prayer for the young minister who had the opening.

Her gaze found the single boys as she searched for Elmer and Roy. Were they behaving? Turning her head, she found her nephews, Allen and Ivan, and yes, there was Roy, whispering to his cousin. Hopefully, he'd remain quiet after he said what he deemed necessary. She'd try to catch his eye to remind him of the fact that she could see him and knew if he misbehaved.

He looked up, guileless as a rabbit, his eyes open wide. Quickly, Ruth sat up straighter, put a finger to her lips, drew down her eyebrows, and shook her head ever so slightly. When Roy, her generally softhearted one, looked as if he would burst into tears, she smiled, only a bit, and gave him a slight wink as a reassurance of her love.

A small smile smoothed out Roy's humiliation, and she felt better, until she looked straight into a pair of very dark brown eyes that didn't turn away from her face. He had seen her wink. There are lots of words for humiliation, but none served to describe her shame.

Oh please don't let him think…. Then the thought struck her that, of course, she had nothing to be ashamed of. He didn't know her, and she had no idea who he was, so they'd never meet again. If he wanted to be so bold as to let her know he was watching, then, well, so be it. Sorry.

She told her sister, Verna, about it after services. They were busy putting red beets and pickles in small Styrofoam bowls to be put on the table with the rest of the traditional food that was served every other Sunday at church.

Verna watched her sister's face—the soft rose of her blush—and tried to laugh. But her mouth took on a squarish quality, and she became quite hysterical as she turned her face away. Her shoulders shook as she cried.

When Verna finished, she lifted her apron and dug out a wrinkled, not-so-white handkerchief and honked mightily into it. Then she lifted red-rimmed eyes to Ruth and said, "Ruth, I don't care if you think I'm not quite right, but you need to think about marrying again someday. Your row is long, and the sun is hot, and you have it tough. I would wish for you a nice and decent young man, a special one for your children."

She again honked her nose into the questionable handkerchief, blinked her eyes, and lifted her apron to return the cloth to her pocket. Then she turned back to the task of fishing sweet pickles out of their brine with a spoon that had no slots in it. Silently, Ruth handed her a slotted spoon. Verna took it, and they finished filling the bowls.

The next time Ruth looked at Verna, she nodded her head ever so slightly, and they shared a watery smile of sisterhood and love and understanding.

Chapter Four

As the late summer sun burned the cool mists of September mornings into glorious fall, the leaves turned slowly into vibrant shades of red, yellow, and orange. The garden was cleared of its tomatoes and brown, rustling cornstalks and diseased marigolds.

Ruth gathered an armload of cornstalks, walked to the white board fence, and flung them over. Then she stood to watch Pete hungrily bite into one, allowing Oatmeal, the small round pony the color of her name, none of the tender evening snack.

"Pete, come on. Stop being greedy. Get over here, Oatmeal. He'll let you have some."

She turned in time to see Roy chasing Barbara across the lawn with a cornstalk held aloft, a banner of intended harm. Barbara was not crying out. She simply lowered her head in determination and outran him, her blue dress flapping as her knees pumped and her brown legs churned. She dodged Roy with the agility of a small rabbit.

Triumphantly and clearly the winner, though her chest was heaving, Barbara turned to face him. Roy swung the cornstalk futilely, accepting defeat, until she charged after him, neatly swiping the offending stalk and racing off with it. Roy took pursuit once more.

Ruth watched, laughing to herself, until Lillian ran directly into Roy's path, where he crashed into her. She fell back, hitting her head on the corner of the wooden sandbox and sending up a series of shrieks and howls, her face turning burgundy, her mouth open wide.

"Stop! No, no, Lillian. Don't cry," Roy said,

bending to help his youngest sister, rubbing her head, sliding her onto his lap as he sat down.

Barbara dropped the cornstalk and came running to see how bad it was. She told Roy it was all his fault, because he had started it. Roy asked who had been running away when this happened, and Barbara retorted that that was not what she had said.

When Ruth reached them, Lillian was still emitting howls of outrage. Good-natured Barbara was bristling with anger, while Roy was determined to prove his point and trying to drive home the blame with his words.

Calm. I will remain calm, Ruth thought. She scooped up Lillian and checked her head for injuries. Her searching fingers found a large goose egg protruding from her daughter's scalp.

"Hush. Hush, Lillian. It's alright," she said softly, which did no good as her words were buried under a fresh supply of howling.

"Roy. Barbara. Stop. Go sit on the bench until you can be quiet."

"It was her!"

"It was Roy!"

"It was not. She started it!"

With Lillian on her hip, Ruth grasped Roy firmly by his shoulder and steered him in the direction of the wooden bench by the back door. Barbara followed, shamefaced.

As she went through the laundry room door, she could hear little Benjamin crying lustily from his playpen, and by the look of his tired, wet face, he had been crying steadily for some time.

Setting Lillian on the couch, Ruth crunched a few saltine crackers beneath her feet as she made her way to Baby Benjy, as they'd come to call him. She had to kick a plastic bucket of toys aside before reaching to extract him from the confines of his playpen.

What was most important here? She put Benjy in his baby swing and pressed the button to set it into motion as she mentally reviewed Lillian's fall, wondering if she should be taken somewhere. The ER was the only service available if she had a serious injury at this time of the evening.

Hadn't she heard somewhere that if a child yells and cries, it's not too serious? Or if a bump appears on the skull? Was that a myth? She could hear her mother saying that if the lump goes in but is not visible on the outside, it can be fatal.

A stab of fear made her cringe, the reality of Lillian's head injury looming ahead of her. She had fifty-seven dollars in her checking account. That was all. The ER would send a bill, and then there was the amount she would have to pay the driver she'd need to hire.

She held Lillian and felt the lump, undecided. She looked up to find Roy and Barbara entering the kitchen, followed by Elmer and Esther, their eyes wide with concern.

"Is she hurt seriously?"

"Is she okay?"

Ruth nodded, assuring them, but she was still unsure about whether Lillian should be seen by a doctor. The last thing she needed was another bill to pay, but her daughter's health was her first priority, she knew.

Oh, Ben.

She held Lillian, and Esther reached for Benjamin, who was not settling down. Ruth maintained a calm appearance as she tried to think rationally while watching Lillian's face, where the color slowly drained away until even her lips were alarmingly pale. What should she do?

She decided to watch her for an hour, then take action. She put a cool washcloth on Lillian's forehead and gave her a dropper filled with children's grape flavored Tylenol. The generic brand at Walmart had been half the price, thank goodness. Lillian swallowed dutifully, sighed, whimpered, and lay very still against her mother's breast.

Don't let them sleep. She could hear her old family doctor's voice as clearly as if he was in the room. Lillian's eyelids sank lower, and Ruth shifted her position to keep her awake.

"Lillian!"

She began to cry.

"Elmer, go get Mamie. Please?"

"Alright."

Instantly, he was out the door. Ruth was thankful for Elmer's obedience and wanted to remember to tell him so.

"Esther, would you please pick up toys? Roy, please get the broom and sweep up these crackers."

They both did her bidding quietly, with reverence for their injured sister worrying them into obedience. Barbara brought a light blanket, and Ruth smiled at her as she covered Lillian's legs.

When Lillian's eyes began to close again, Ruth sat her up, saying, "Lillian!"

She was immensely grateful to see her neighbor, Mamie Stoltzfus, wife of Ephraim, come through the front door with her youngest, Waynie, hanging haphazardly on her plump hip. His thin blond hair was matted, his nose running, his blue eyes alight with interest—a small replica of his mother.

Mamie was what Ruth lovingly called "roly-poly." She was a heavy woman, though tall, with thinning hair and bright blue eyes. She viewed the world through rosy lenses, an extension of her heart overflowing with love and compassion toward every person she had the pleasure of knowing.

"*Ach* (oh) my, Ruth."

She bent to look at Lillian with Waynie bobbing along on her hip. She felt the large lump, stepped back to look at Lillian's face, and lifted the eyelids to look for contraction in the pupils. Then she clucked.

Ruth was assailed by odors of cooking and baking, twice weekly baths, Waynie's unchanged cloth diaper, and other smells associated with Mamie's relaxed approach to life.

"What happened? Here, Waynie, you sit here. Look, there's a car. You want to play with the toys? Look, there's a teddy!"

Waynie gurgled happily and crawled across the floor, his questionable odor following him. Mamie grunted and straightened her substantial frame before sitting down beside Ruth, who promptly leaned against her as the cushions flattened under Mamie.

"The children were playing and knocked her over. She hit her head against the corner of the sandbox. She really cried."

"Oh, she looks aright. Some color's coming back to her cheeks. *Gel*, Lillian? *Gel, doo bisht alright. Gel?* (Right, you will be fine. Right?)"

Nodding and smiling, Maime reached for her neighbor's daughter, her arms and hands and heart needing to be about their business. She gathered Lillian against her greasy dress front and kissed her cheek.

"*Bisht falla?* (Did you fall?)"

Suddenly, Lillian sat straight up and said, "I broke my head apart."

"You did? Just like Humpty Dumpty?"

Lillian nodded and giggled, watching Waynie crawl in pursuit of a rolling ball. She pushed against Mamie's red hands and slid off her lap. She walked steadily over to Waynie and patted his bottom, giggling.

Tears sprang to Ruth's eyes, and her knees became weak with relief. Mamie beamed and said Lillian had quite a bump there but by all appearances would be fine.

"You wouldn't have a doctor examine her?"

"No. She just had a good tap on her head."

"Tap?"

Ruth shook her head, laughing.

As the sun made a glorious exit behind the oak tree, Mamie settled herself into a kitchen chair with a cup of hot spearmint tea and a plate of chocolate peanut butter bars.

"You didn't need to do this," she chortled happily, immensely pleased at the prospect of visiting with Ruth.

"No, no, it's okay. I need something to pick me up after that scare," Ruth assured her.

"I can't imagine life without Ephraim," Mamie said, quick tears of sympathy appearing in her happy eyes.

Ruth nodded, then sent the older children out to finish the removal of the cornstalks. After they'd gone, she turned to Mamie.

"It's not always easy, although I can't complain. I have so much to be thankful for, in so many ways."

Mamie dipped a bar into her heavily sugared tea, then clucked in dismay when it broke apart and the wet part disappeared into the hot liquid. Quickly, Ruth was on her feet to get a spoon, but Mamie held one up, laughing, and fished the wet particles out of the tea.

"Drowned my chocolate chip bar! Oh well."

She slurped mightily as she bit into another half of a bar. She nodded her head in appreciation and shook her spoon in Ruth's direction as she chewed, an indication of the volley of words that was to follow.

"I don't know how you do it. Everything so neat and clean. Your work is always done. You just glide seamlessly through your days and never complain. Waynie, no. Don't. As I was saying, how can you handle all your children, and get your work done? Waynie, no."

She heaved herself off the chair and extracted her young son from a potted plant, as Ruth winced at the trail of potting soil spreading across the linoleum, which was apparently invisible to Mamie.

Mamie settled Waynie on her lap and began feeding him chunks of the chocolate chip bar.

"You know Mert Ordwich died?"

"Who?"

"Mert. You know, the feed salesman. Oh, I forgot. You're not on the farm. Well, he had hardening of the arteries and wouldn't go to the doctor. That's how thick headed he was. Ephraim says he's stubborn as a mule. He was. I doubt if he is now anymore. We went to his viewing last night. The line was so long, and my feet hurt so bad. There we stood and stood, on and on. He didn't look like Mert. His face was so puffy."

Mamie looked at Lillian.

"She seems perfectly alright. Anyway... Waynie, *komm*. As I was saying, they say the David Petersheim place is sold. Eli Kings were standing in line with us. They said a young bachelor bought it. We…I don't know if he's a bachelor. I shouldn't say. He's single, but he's going with Paul King's Anna."

Ruth chuckled.

"He's single, but he's dating?"

Mamie laughed uproariously and thumped the table solidly in a most unladylike manner. Ruth watched her and felt her spirits lifting. She was also relieved knowing Lillian would be alright, and she was glad.

"*Ach* Ruth, I'm getting old. I say the dumbest things. You know what I mean. He's pretty old—to be unmarried. Anyway, he must have money, or his father does, paying four hundred and some thousand."

Mamie paused as she reached for another cookie bar.

"I'll just eat this one, and then I have to go. Oh, I meant to ask you. We have a shopping trip planned at the end of October—early Christmas shopping. Would you want to go with me and a few others?"

Ruth simply didn't know what to say. How could she respond honestly and yet keep her pride intact at the same time? So she hesitated, pulled Lillian onto her lap, and checked the lump on her head to buy time. Then she answered Mamie.

"I'll see."

"Good! Oh, I hope you can go! We'd love to have you."

Later that night, when the late September moon had risen above the oak tree and bathed the small house in a soft, white glow, Ruth lay in her king sized bed, her eyes wide, her mind churning with endless questions and possibilities. What to do?

No one was aware of the state of her bank account. No one would need to know. Times were difficult for many people. They all had enough to do, simply staying afloat, paying mortgages, and providing for their own large families.

"*Arme vitve, vine nicht* (Poor widow, do not cry)."

Is that really what she was? How had it happened? How had she been toppled from her pedestal as Ben's loving wife? Toppled and broken into a million pieces. Would she ever find a way out of this labyrinth of personal fear of failure? Could she survive financially, as a lone parent, raising these fast growing and maturing children? And these boys. They so desperately needed a father figure in their lives.

Well, the fifty-seven dollars would hold them a few weeks. Then she'd either have to beg from her parents, or…or what?

The quilt was almost finished. She had four hundred yards of thread in it so far. At seventy-five cents a yard, that would be three hundred dollars. The gas bill was almost a hundred and forty dollars, and the telephone maybe fifty or sixty.

She'd go to B. B.'s Store, the bent and dent grocery in Quarryville. If she was especially careful, she could make do on seventy or eighty dollars.

The horse feed was about all gone. Well, they'd have to wait till another quilt was finished. In a few more years, the boys would be fourteen and fifteen and able to earn a few dollars, but until then…she didn't know.

She rolled on her side and punched her pillow into a different shape. Then she stretched out her arm, her fingers searching for Lillian's small form, and checked the rise and fall of her daughter's breath, feeling that comforting, even rhythm that assured Ruth she was alright.

Mamie was a treasure, asking her to go Christmas shopping with the others. Should Ruth have been honest with her? So far, she had no clue how they would celebrate Christmas—with gifts, anyway. Perhaps this year she would tell the children they would receive gifts from their grandparents and the teacher at school, but since their dat was no longer here, they wouldn't have Christmas gifts at home.

How could she manage?

Elmer and Esther would understand. She

pictured Elmer with his shoulders held too high and his hands in his pockets, the "little man" stance he'd developed in the past five months. Ruth ached with love for her eldest son.

How could she—if she had a chance—replace Ben? How did one go about procuring a replacement for a husband? She guessed she couldn't. At least not outwardly.

There came a time, though, when she had to wonder what God had in store. Did He think it was best to stay alone? Was there anyone who would even consider taking the wild leap into the chaotic lives of six children and their mother?

She remembered the emotion her sister, Verna, had shown. But that Vern was something else—slightly unstable. Ruth thought of the wrinkled, yellowing handkerchief, knowing it wasn't laundered properly and had never seen an iron.

None of the sisters knew why Verna was that way. Verna herself claimed she was adopted. She didn't care one whit about her yard or garden or housework. She bought all her canned goods at

B. B.'s Store in Quarryville, saying she could buy them cheaper than she could can them herself.

She pieced quilts and bought Little Debbies for her children, or Nutter Butters or Chips Ahoy. Her oldest, named Ellen—Mam had a fit about that fancy name—did the washing just as fast as she could without paying much attention to the outcome.

The thought of her sister and her questionable laundry was the deciding factor between sleep and more tumbling thoughts of worry. Ruth barely had time to pull Lillian's softly breathing form against her own before giving into asleep.

Chapter Five

RUTH WALKED TOWARD THE HOUSE, LEAFING through her mail as the October wind caught her skirt and whipped it around her knees. The gas bill, a few cards from folks in the community who remembered to send lines of encouragement—sometimes containing crisp twenty dollar bills—some junk mail, an offer for a credit card, which was tempting.

Hmm.

A letter with no stamp? Without her full address? She struggled to pull the storm door completely shut and then laid the mail on the kitchen table before hanging her black sweater on the row of hooks by the wringer washer.

Shivering, she sat down to open her mail. She found nothing unusual, but she was grateful for the cards with the usual verses, a token of care sent by people she did not know.

She saved the one without a stamp for last, somehow savoring the mystery of it. She blinked and caught her breath. The envelope contained a plain sheet of notebook paper from an ordinary composition book with the loose fragments of paper still hanging from the holes where it had been torn from the notebook.

One, two, three….She almost stopped counting as her heart started beating wildly in her chest. Ten. There were ten one hundred dollar bills. There was no greeting and no name.

She hadn't planned on crying. It just happened, starting with her nostrils burning and a huge lump in her throat that was relieved only when the splash of tears began. She folded her arms on top of the mail on the oak table and let the wonder of this generous gift overtake her.

"Mam?"

Elmer's concern forced her to lift her head. She felt guilty now to be indulging in these senseless tears.

"I'm sorry, Elmer."

"What's wrong?"

Silently she handed the money to him and watched through blurred vision as he counted, then whistled softly.

"We're rich!"

"What?! What?!"

Roy came bouncing over with Barbara at his heels. That was the one thing Ruth would never understand—the way Barbara did that, always going where Roy went, only to be constantly irritated by his antics.

"Somebody gave us a bunch of money!"

"Let me see."

It was October eleventh, the day most Amish people set aside as a day of fasting and prayer in order to prepare themselves for the fall communion services. Ruth had always relished this rare day of relaxation to spend with Ben and the children. The day was an uninterrupted one, sanctioned for the reading of the German articles of faith or the prayer book, the traditional books read and re-read by generations of Old Order Amish.

There was no breakfast for Ruth on fasting day, but she prepared buttered toast and Honey Nut Cheerios for the children. Lillian, of course, refused them, saying she wanted Trix. In her frustration, Lillian kicked the bench from her perch on the blue plastic booster seat and cried, squeezing her eyes shut and turning her head from side to side until the other children laughed at her. Then she lifted her face with her eyes closed and just howled because they were laughing, and Ruth had to shush the older ones. She took Lillian away from the table and talked to her firmly, saying there were no Trix in the house and if she wouldn't eat Cheerios, she would have nothing at all and would be just like the three little pigs who were lazy and the wolf blew their house away.

That made Lillian sit up straight and open her eyes. She told Ruth that a wolf could not blow houses away, but the story had served to get her mind off the Trix. She ate her Cheerios, and general peace was restored.

Ruth read her *Luscht Gartlein* (Love Garden), her soul blossoming and unfolding, as it received the simple German words about the wise ways one could live a good and Godly life. The reading of the German took more of her time, but she savored the pronunciation and the meaning of these words, remembering the agelessness of them.

At noon, she fried corn meal mush, cutting the squares from the aluminum cake pan and frying them in vegetable oil. It was Elmer's favorite for *fasht dag* (fast day) lunch. Ruth heated milk in a small saucepan and then poured it over a bowl full of saltines and covered them with a plate while she fried eggs.

Esther set the table, adding salt and pepper, ketchup, butter, and strawberry jelly to the spread with plates, knives, and forks. There was no

orange juice, and grapes had been too expensive
to can juice, so they drank cold water for their
lunch on *fasht dag*.

When Ruth bowed her head before they ate,
she remembered to thank God especially for the
gift of one thousand dollars that had come with
the early morning mail delivery.

The cornmeal mush was delicious. The boys
devoured every last slice and ate two eggs each
and all the buttered toast they could hold.

Esther didn't like mush, so she wrinkled her
nose and said it was greasy and disgusting. Elmer
said that was great if she didn't eat it so he'd have
more. Roy nodded his head in agreement, his
straight brown hair sliding back and forth with
each movement.

Esther said just doddies (grandfathers) and
mommies ate mush. Roy said they did not either.
Anyone could eat mush if they felt like it.

Esther said rich people ate bacon, and Elmer
said they *were* rich. Roy nodded his head again.
Esther looked at Ruth and said, "Right, Mam,

we're not rich?"

"We are rich, Esther. We have each other and God takes very good care of us."

After that wonderful *fasht dag*, the coal bin was filled with three tons of coal, the gas bill was paid, and Ruth planned to go Christmas shopping with Mamie.

A few days before the shopping trip, the boys hitched Oatmeal to the cart and went back to the farm for two gallons of milk. It was a gray sort of day, chilly and overcast with the clouds bulging with rain that hadn't started to fall. Elmer said later that was why he didn't see the oncoming truck—it was gray, too.

Ruth saw the whole thing from the kitchen window and clutched Benjamin with one hand as she clapped the other across her mouth to stifle a scream. She was completely helpless as she watched Elmer pull out directly in front of a pickup truck. She saw him come down hard with the leather reins on the pony's haunches, scaring poor Oatmeal out of her wits. The driver also hit the brakes, and Oatmeal lunged forward, spilling both boys out onto the road.

Roy came screaming and crying, completely beside himself with pain and fear and holding his left wrist with his right hand. Ruth laid crying Benjy into his playpen and asked Esther to watch him, please. She'd be back.

The driver of the truck was middle aged, lean, and sensible but most definitely shaken up and unhappy with his circumstances at that moment. Elmer was running down the road after his surprised pony, Roy was yelling senselessly, and some very black tire marks stretched along Hoosier Road. But thank God, no one was seriously injured.

The driver's name was Dan Rogers, and he offered to call the police, although his truck wasn't damaged. Ruth grasped her sweater at the waistline and shivered as her teeth chattered. She told him it was fine, she'd have the wrist checked by their family doctor.

Dan stayed long enough to watch Roy spread

his fingers, lift and lower his hand, and rotate his wrist. Then he waited until Elmer returned with Oatmeal and the cart, apparently unharmed, although Elmer had telltale streaks of gray where he'd wiped fiercely at his little boy tears.

Ruth hugged both boys together, gathering them close in a thankful embrace. That night she spent a very restless night as Roy woke up continually, calling for his mother because of the pain.

In the morning, resignedly, she took Roy to Intercourse to Doctor Pfieffer, who did a quick diagnosis and said it was only a bad sprain as the x-ray showed no fracture. He put a splint on the wrist and wrapped it over and over.

Ruth wrote out a check for two hundred and fifteen dollars, signed her name, and took Roy home again. She settled him on the couch with a few books and then took Benjamin and walked down the road to Mamie's house. Ruth knocked on the front door and was greeted by the usual insane yipping of Mamie's brown Pomeranian.

Mamie opened the door, a men's handkerchief

of a questionable cleanliness tied around her head, a torn bib apron sliding off one shoulder, and Waynie, as usual, stuck on one hip like a permanent fixture.

"I don't know why you think you always have to knock," she said as her way of greeting Ruth.

"It's polite, Mamie."

"Who's polite? What is that? Here, give me your precious bundle. Waynie, go play now. Trixie, shoo. *Gay*! (Go!) Waynie, Trixie!"

Waynie sat down and howled. Trixie continued yipping, and Benjamin's eyes grew very wide and uncertain.

"*Ach* my! My house is a total circus. Johnny, come get Trixie. Put her in the *kesslehaus*. Fannie, come get Waynie. Susan, where's Fannie? Well, here, Susan, give him a graham cracker in his high chair. Trixie! Johnny! Come get this dog!"

Ruth couldn't stop smiling, the warmth spreading through her like bright, summer sunshine. She loved Mamie so much she wanted to send her a card with a funny saying about friends or a bouquet of flowers, but as it was, she knew she could afford neither, so she unwrapped Benjamin and handed him to an eager Fannie. She was Mamie's oldest daughter, tall and slim, with a splattering of freckles and brown eyes. She had magically appeared after Susan, her younger blonde-haired sister, had taken away the wailing Waynie.

"He's teething," Mamie sighed.

"Poor Waynie, he looks unhappy."

"He is."

"Well, Mamie, I came to tell you that I'll have to back out of the shopping trip. The boys had a near accident yesterday, pulling out in front of a pickup with Oatmeal, and I had to have Roy's wrist taken care of."

"Oh no! Are they okay?"

"Yes, just a bad sprain in Roy's left wrist."

"Well, good, but it really spites me you can't go with us. Do you want me to give you some money? Of course, I better not say that. Eph would have a fit. He can hardly get forty hours in down at the shed place, this time of year. Trixie!"

Mamie got up and lumbered after the tiny Pomeranian. Ruth had to wonder what kept the dog alive, being underfoot all the time.

"I don't know where that Johnny is. Now, as we were saying, if you can't go, will you be able to have Christmas gifts this year? *Ach* Ruth, I simply pity you so bad. I'm going to tell Davey that you're out of money."

"No! Mamie please. Our deacon has enough to think about."

"You want coffee?"

"No, I have to get back. Roy might need me."

Ruth glanced around, trying not to notice the piles of dirty dishes, the messy stove top, the fly hanger above the table dotted with dead houseflies—not to mention the clutter all over the floor.

"Stop looking at my house."

Ruth laughed. With Mamie, everything was easy. You could always be yourself and say what you wanted without having to attempt any unnecessary niceties.

"Why don't you wash your dishes?"

"You know why?"

"Why?"

"Because I don't like washing dishes. Ever. I have to force myself to tackle a sink load of them. They need to come up with a dishwasher that runs on air."

"Tell Ephraim to start designing one. He could."

"Ppfff!"

Ruth smiled and then laughed.

"Mamie, you are the dearest best friend in the world. I just have to tell you how much I appreciate you."

"*Ach* Ruth, now you're going to make me cry. Well, I feel the same about you. Just so you know." Then Mamie held her head to one side, eyed Ruth shrewdly, and asked if she loved her enough to wash dishes.

"I'd love to wash your dishes."

"I bet."

Still smiling, Ruth walked home, richer in

friendship than in money. That was sure.

All through the rest of the month of October, Ruth tried not to plan ahead unnecessarily or build up mountains of worry.

Of course, Mam and the sisters planned shopping trips for November, in between weddings and all the usual events planned around them.

Ruth had received three wedding invitations. She put them back in the envelopes slowly, absentmindedly letting her fingers trace the embossed lettering.

How could she attend a wedding alone? If ever there was a single event that would cripple her sense of being even slightly courageous, it had to be a wedding. How could she endure a whole day surrounded by couples, dating ones or married ones? The absence of Ben was a painful handicap, even just thinking about it.

No, she would not go.

Chicken pox spread through the community all through November. The boys went to school as usual, having had them when they were much younger, but Esther and Barbara were feverish, achy, and irritable. They argued and fought over toys and crayons and books. And relentless, cold rain pounded against the east windows, ran down the panes, and puddled between the wet, swaying bushes. The bare branches of the old oak tree looked cold and black and slick, etched against the weeping sky.

Benjamin fussed in his swing. Lillian somehow found a permanent marker and scribbled all over the hallway, and Ruth felt as if she would not be able to tolerate one more day alone without Ben.

The pustules from the chicken pox broke out all over the girls' little bodies, and they finally felt better. When they became itchy, Ruth patiently filled the bathtub with warm water, added baking soda, swirled it around well, and let the girls play in the tub.

She scrubbed the hallway walls with Comet and Soft Scrub, but a faint gray line remained. Well, it would have to stay that way. There was no money for paint. She could ask Mam, she supposed, but she was always asking her for things like mantles for the propane lamp or batteries or rubber bands, things she never quite had enough money to buy.

But it's my life, she thought, as she sat rocking little Benjamin after she had rubbed his gums with teething lotion and given him a good hot bath and some Tylenol. Poor baby, she thought. He couldn't help it if those hard, little teeth pushed against his soft, tender gums and made them ache.

She wrapped him in a warm blanket and inhaled the smell of him, that sweet baby lotion smell that never failed to bring her joy.

When he was asleep, she laid him in his crib with a soft, white cloth diaper spread over the crib sheet, just in case he threw up during the night. She covered him to his ears and then folded the comforter back so she could kiss him one more time before tiptoeing out.

Lillian was lying on the couch, her pacifier in her mouth, her eyes wide and anxious as they always were when she felt sleep trying to overtake her, though she desperately tried to avoid it.

"*Komm*, Lillian."

Gratefully, Ruth gathered her three year old in her arms, savoring the comforting routine of smoothing the flannel nightgown, taut and neat, over the rounded little form. She did love her mighty Lillian, so pliant and adorable now.

"*Bisht meet* (Are you tired), Lillian?"

She nodded, her eyes wide.

"Shall I sing?"

"No."

"Why not?"

"I don't want you to. I want my Dat."

"But Lillian, your Dat is in Heaven."

"No, he isn't."

"Yes. His part that is alive went to Heaven—his soul."

Softly, Lillian began to cry, but Ruth remained strong, showing no emotion of her own. Soon, Lillian stopped crying and went to sleep. Tomorrow was another day, and she'd forget. Till the next time.

Ruth held the warm, sleeping form. Outside she heard the wind rattling the downspout at the corner of the house and playing with the loose shutter by the front door. She hoped the boys had remembered to close the barn door after they'd fed Pete.

She stroked Lillian's *schtruvvels* (stray hairs) away from her face and prayed for strength to carry on.

Chapter Six

The Thanksgiving hymn singing was to be held in Ephraim's shop, and Mamie was a complete wreck for an entire week beforehand. She waved her arms and almost yodeled with apprehension. Daily life overwhelmed her, let alone cleaning that shop and getting all that coffee going.

"I know just how this will go. Everyone says, oh they'll bring bars and cookies and potato chips and cheese and all the dips and pretzels and stuff, but what do they bring? I'm going to bake my Christmas cookies now. All of 'em, just in case it goes the same way it did last year. Why in the world that husband of mine offered, I'll never know. He knows I don't get around the way some women do."

But she was pleased to be an important member of the community, hosting this hymn singing for the youth and their parents, or some of them, as it usually turned out.

Ruth walked home with a promise to return to help bake cookies, something she genuinely anticipated. She enjoyed being in Mamie's company. The cookies, too, would be phenomenal, she knew.

Mamie mostly did what she liked, and baking was at the top of her list. Her specialty was raisin-filled sugar cookies. She used an old, old recipe that had been handed down for generations. She also used fillings other than just raisin—raspberry, blueberry, cherry, even lemon—and they melted away in one bite.

So the week flew by with Ruth helping Mamie and joking with her friend's good-natured husband. As he sat dipping cookies in milk, he seemed happily oblivious to the unbelievable mess around them.

They filled the sugar cookies with the various kinds of fruit fillings. Then they baked oatmeal raisin and chocolate chip cookies and date pinwheels. They made gingersnaps and molasses cookies with one side dipped in white chocolate. Mamie wanted to make chocolate cut out cookies, but Ruth refused, saying the singing was only three days away and when did she think she was going to clean?

Mamie plunked herself down on a flour-dusted kitchen chair and said she'd never get ready, that was all there was to it. Ruth eyed her neighbor's girth and imagined every extra movement of hers was balanced by plenty of extra calories. She'd guarantee Mamie had eaten ten cookies in the past few hours. It was actually scary.

"You know you're going to become diabetic?"

"What? Me?"

Mamie was horrified, till Ruth assured her she was joking. In truth, she wasn't completely.

At the end of the day, the smells, the sounds,

and bustle of baking at Mamie's house put Ruth's home in stark contrast as she headed back with her tired children to a cold, dark house, the absence of Ben felt in every room. She'd stoke the coal stove in the basement, light the warm propane lamp, and bravely go ahead for the children's sake, getting them to bed without fights as best she could.

Thanksgiving was spent with her family, a day of feasting on roast turkey and sweet potato casserole, surround by all of her dear family with every face a homecoming for her spirit.

Mam glided smoothly between stovetop and table, serving and barking orders. Her daughters scuttled to obey, pushing children aside in the process.

Twelve o'clock was not allowed to arrive until everyone was seated, the water poured, and heads bent in prayer. As always, Mam accomplished her goal and even ahead of time—the long hand on the clock pointing to the ten, the short hand to the twelve.

The children had a great time at Doddy

(Grandfather) Lapp's, but anticipation ran high to continue their wonderful day at Ephraim's. They put Pete in the barn at home, unharnessed him, and fed him a good amount of oats and hay. In the house, they stoked the fire, washed a few faces, combed hair, dabbed at a few spots on the girls' pinafore-style aprons, and waited till Roy dashed to his room to change into a pair of black school trousers—he had spilled gravy all over his legs. Then they were off down the road to the neighbors' Thanksgiving hymn singing.

The wind was spiked with wet coldness, the forerunner of a chilly November rain, so they wasted no time getting to the brightly lit shop at Ephraim's. Buggies were being parked with teams approaching from either direction, so Ruth huddled the children to the side of the road, out of the way of approaching hooves and steel wheels.

She could always tell the difference between the young men's teams and the teams belonging to families. The youth drove horses with plenty of speed or style, sometimes both, and their harnesses were decked out in flashes of silver or chrome. The battery-powered lights on their buggies also outnumbered those of their parents, whose teams had only the necessary headlights, blinking orange taillights, and the reflective, slow-moving vehicle emblem—a triangle of orange in obedience to Pennsylvania laws of the road.

Often the youth decorated their slow-moving vehicle signs with stickers from amusement parks or their favorite football teams, which was tolerated in varying degrees. Some older members of the community smiled knowingly, while others frowned.

The shop at Ephraim's was a haven of warmth and light. Some of the glossy church benches had been set on trestles to form a long table with the remaining benches on either side and the German songbooks stacked neatly along the makeshift table.

Off to the side, Mamie had set up two folding tables end to end and covered them with her good tablecloths. Then she had loaded them with Tupperware containers and plastic ice cream buckets full of her Christmas cookies. Large containers each held five gallons of piping hot coffee, and there was Coffee-mate creamer and sugar and a basket containing napkins and plastic spoons all set out in a manageable order.

Bags of pretzels and potato chips, deep bowls of homemade Chex Mix, platters of cheese and German ring bologna, dips and vegetables—loads of food appeared as if by magic as happy, festive women offered their contributions and delivered them to their proper places on Mamie's tables.

"Ruth!" Mamie bore down on her, a locomotive of suppressed energy bristling with excitement.

"Mamie! Everything looks so nice. Your table is all decked out, and the coffee ready. You must have worked hard."

"Oh, I did. I'm ready to drop. Then Waynie was a mess with his teething, and Fannie had to go wash for Elam *sei* Katie. She has Lyme disease, you know. Hiya, Benjamin! Hiya. Come here, you sweet bundle. Oh Ruth, he's so cute. *Gel*, Benjy? Hi, Lillian. How's her head? *Komm*, Lillian. I want to see your head. *Gooka-mol* (Let me see)."

Lillian stood stock-still as Mamie's fingers explored the surface of the little skull, her eyes lifted solemnly to Mamie's kind face.

"The bump went away now, so it's better," she announced solemnly.

"*Ach ya, gel?*"

Mamie sat down, unwrapped little Benjamin, took Lillian's proffered coat, and left Ruth to search the room for other familiar faces.

The men were assembling on folding chairs, their beards wagging as they talked. They were dressed in colorful shirts, pastel blues and beiges with an occasional navy or burgundy. They smiled as they greeted one another with firm handshakes or familiar claps on the shoulder.

Ruth turned away, the loss of Ben—the raw absence of him—so unbearable when his brother, Sam, arrived. He smiled, then caught her eye and waved. So much like Ben. No one could ever replace his memory, she knew now. That knowledge was engraved into her being, like the words that were etched on his perfect gravestone.

"Ruth, what? A shadow just passed across your face. You're missing Ben, *gel*? *Ach* my, Ruth. Maybe you shouldn't have come. You poor thing. I can't stand it. *Komm, sits ana* (sit down)."

Mamie slipped a heavy arm around Ruth's drooping form, and the hurt was replaced by her friend's pure kindness along with the scent of her lack of a good antiperspirant—the only blight on their friendship. Ruth had never worked up the audacity to mention it. She winced now but resigned herself and chose to accept the kindness, regardless of the less than fresh Mamie.

"It's okay. I'm just being childish," Ruth whispered.

The two greeted others who came by to shake hands, give an occasional hug, and offer words of friendliness. They asked how she was, always. And always, Ruth would smile and say, "*Goot* (Good)," nod her head, and hope the person holding her hand would believe it.

No, I'm not always *goot*. My money is all but gone once again, Lillian is driving me batty, and I miss Ben so much right this minute, I could just run home and wrap up in a blanket and turn my face to the wall. My spigot leaks—the one in the laundry room—and a section of spouting is loose. So don't ask me how I am, because I'll just have to put on that false veneer of shining goodness that comes from generation after generation of pasted smiles and hidden suffering.

Ruth knew the Amish were always expected to be *goot*. It is bred in them, this taking up of their crosses, bowing of their heads, and repetition of "Thy will be done." They carry on, and when the load becomes unbearable, they still endure it. It is the Amish way. The Lord giveth, and the Lord taketh away. Ruth allowed a small sigh to escape.

As the girls filed in, shaking hands and greeting the women with polite smiles, Ruth turned her attention to look with interest at the different colors and styles of the dresses as well as the hairstyles. She noted which ones were neat and which could use a little work.

How well she remembered the anticipation of each hymn singing when she was young. Would this be the evening Ben would notice her? Would he be seated close by or much too far away toward the other end of the table?

Always, there had been Ben. She was fifteen when she spoke to him that first time. She'd fallen hard and had never been the same. It was at a volleyball game on a lovely summer evening. She was not yet sixteen, so she wasn't actually *rumspringing*, but he'd come over to her and Rachel and said, "Hello, Ruth, how are you?"

Their time together had been so short, and yet her mind was packed with many memories of their love. It remained a wondrous thing to file away those golden mental files that hung neatly in her special place labeled "Marriage, a heaven on earth." For she had loved him, given herself to him, and adored the ground he walked on.

Could she ever love again, in that same way?

No. A steely resolve closed her heart to the thought. It seemed wrong somehow. She felt sure Ben would not want her to consider a second love.

You need to care for our children, Ruth.

Ruth blinked, frightened, her eyes wide. Who had spoken?

She looked left, then right, and then straight ahead and directly into the deep brown eyes of that bachelor who was single but dating Anna— Paul King's Anna. Ruth tried to look away, but she was held by his gaze that was asking her questions again.

How can eyes speak? she wondered much later that night. Those eyes had asked, Who are you, Ruth? How can I ever get to know you?

At the moment, because she had felt flushed and brazen and was still pondering whose voice she had heard speaking to her about the children, she had finally lowered her head. Her downcast eyes and the heavy lashes sweeping her softly blushing cheeks—none of it was lost on Mamie, who sat straight up and blinked. She pursed her lips, clasped her hands firmly in her lap, and knew.

The singing rose and fell. The lovely old hymns of the forefathers were coupled with choruses of English songs as the men's deep voices blended in complete harmony with the lighter tones of the women.

Ruth cuddled Benjamin, bent over him, and kissed his downy cheeks as she pondered her explosion of emotion, masked, of course, by her steadiness of character.

The coffee was piping hot, and the assortment of cookies and bars and pretzels and cheese and popcorn passed from person to person in a steady stream as the voices of young and old raised in cheery banter during the fellowship that always followed *an shoene singin* (a nice singing).

Eventually the horses were brought and attached to cold buggies, the headlights illuminating the person connecting the britchments and leather pulls to shafts. Friends called out their well wishes, and a few men hurried to help an insecure sixteen year old with a rowdy, misbehaving horse.

This was common on cold, late evenings when the horses were tired of standing tied side by side in unfamiliar barns or along cold fences.

Ruth hurried the children along, careful to hold Benjamin close, warning Elmer to keep hold of Lillian's hand.

Suddenly a dark figure emerged and stepped in front of her, blocking her way.

She stopped, hesitant.

A deep, craggy voice spoke out of the blackness.

"May I ask your name?" He was breathing too fast.

Startled, not thinking, she said quickly, "Ruth Miller."

"These are your children?"

"Yes."

"Sorry if I appear rude. I'm John Beiler."

He extended a hand. Ruth shifted Benjamin, found the stranger's hand, and shook it politely.

"I would offer a ride, but I think your house is not far away."

"No."

"John!"

An irritated voice broke through the stillness as a tall, dark figure appeared, threw herself at John, and clasping his hand and looking up into his face, said, "Where were you? I've been ready to go for a long time."

"I'm sorry."

Nodding his head at Ruth, he moved off, firmly pulled along by his fiancé, evidently, leaving Ruth shaking her head at the boldness of girls in this modern day.

Ruth couldn't fall asleep. She finally got up, took down the flashlight that hung from the hook in the pantry, and found the trustworthy bottle of Tylenol P.M. Sleeping pills or not, sometimes they were a necessity to help her cope with the problems as they approached. Lack of rest was her biggest hurdle. She had learned that the hard way.

Thoughts tumbled about, turning a labyrinth of normal thinking into a hopeless puzzle. Why had she heard that? Those words? Were angels among us, she prayed. Please God, why? "You need to care for our children." As if it were Ben. It wasn't his voice, exactly, but more like a loud thought. Or a thought out loud. Was she losing her mind?

And those eyes. Oh, dear God. She was so ashamed. But, yes, they were like Ben's. Too much so. Heavenly Father, please keep me from falling in love. It's wrong for me, now.

In the morning, when Roy went to feed Pete and Oatmeal, he came back immediately, saying there was a box on the porch, a banana box, the kind they got from B. B.'s Store.

Quickly, Ruth lowered her hands from brushing Esther's hair, telling her to wait, and hurried after Roy. She lifted off the lid of cardboard box with its blue and yellow writing.

A hand went to her throat. Roy was the first to look, turning the large John Martin's ham on its side, touching the Butterball turkey, and poking at the large bundle wrapped in white butcher paper.

"Mam! Look! A turkey! What's in the paper?

Let's take it to the kitchen table."

Elmer joined them, and the boys strained to lift the box with Ruth's help. Esther and Barbara stretched on their tiptoes, peering in to see for themselves as Ruth unwrapped the white parcel. There was a mound of fresh ground sausage, and her mouth watered thinking of the crisp fried patties she could make to eat with scrambled eggs.

The ham was enormous, and already she planned to bake it, freeze portions of it, and make soup and homemade potpie and ham salad. Oh, the wonder of it! Christmas was all taken care of now, at least the dinner here at home.

There was another package of ground beef and one of chicken breast—something she had not bought since Ben died. She would marinate it and then sauté it for only a few minutes—so good. She'd make a wonderful pot of chicken corn noodle soup with chunks of celery and slivers of carrot and parsley.

"Oh my goodness!" Barbara exclaimed.

"We're going to eat like kings!" Esther said and

went twirling around the kitchen, her skirts flying in a circle around her and her partially done hair in disarray.

Lillian gave a whoop of pure excitement and followed, copying every move of her older sister.

Elmer, however, looked very grave as he pinched his mouth into a serious line, his eyes concerned. "How do we know who left it? How do we know it's safe?" he asked.

Ruth stopped. She noticed the way he held his shoulders, so erect, so…just so much more mature than his age with responsibility weighing on the thin boyish shoulders long before they were round enough or strong enough to support it. It broke her heart, the way he felt he needed to protect them—her oldest child and yet still so vulnerable.

"Listen, Elmer, I do understand your point. There is always that danger. But we need to have faith in our fellow humans. I think it was given to us by someone who was directed by God to do so. I think it's good, clean, wonderful food. Can you imagine our Christmas dinner with all of this?"

She smiled widely, held up one palm, and raised her eyebrows in question. Elmer nodded, grinned, and then sidled up to give her a resounding high five, followed by a leaping Roy who slapped her palm so hard she cradled it with her other hand and faked a serious injury.

"Hooo-boy!"

Barbara and Esther giggled and laughed before they caught sight of the clock and shrieked.

"Ten to eight!"

"Oh my goodness!"

That day the children went to school after shoveling cold cereal into their mouths at the very last minute. They rushed out the door still pulling on their coats and smacking their hats onto their heads before racing down the road on their scooters. Their journey to school that day was filled with more merriment than they'd had since their father passed away.

Chapter Seven

WHO HAD DONE IT, THOUGH? SOMEONE with plenty of common sense and knowledge of a poor widow's needs, Ruth thought.

The banana box of delicious meat was soon followed by another one that was mysteriously delivered on the same night Lillian became terribly ill with a sore throat. How could a mother be rocking her child in the living room with the blinds halfway up and not see someone leave a box outside in plain view?

Lillian was so sick, her little body racked with pain and fever that no amount of Tylenol would touch. It was a long night with an abundance of fear and unanswered questions. The small kerosene lamp by the recliner provided a small, steady flame of reassurance, while the shadows along the wall brought doubt and sorrow. The flickering gloominess reflected Ruth's constantly shifting emotions as Lillian's little heart pounded in her thin, little chest and her breathing became shallow and ragged. The little patient repeatedly cried out in pain when she tried to swallow.

Mam arrived in the morning, an angel quickly transported by an English driver. Her blue eyes filled with tears of understanding as she carried in her Unkers salve, Infection Aid, and liquid Vitamin C along with her knowledge of onion poultices and vinegar baths.

As always, Ruth meant to stay strong, but her resolve crumbled the minute she met with the kindness in her mother's eyes. She handed Lillian over to Mommy, soothed a crying Benjamin, and knew it was time to admit she wasn't *goot*. She was completely overwhelmed and underfunded. And, yes, she had bought those two rugs at Walmart, but now her money was all gone, and she just wanted to buy Christmas gifts and be normal with a husband who provided for her.

She did not want to be the poor widow who people watched with sympathy and pity. She wanted to hold up her head and say, "Stop it. I am Ruth. I am still human, and I want to be accepted as one of you and laugh when I want to or say silly things if I feel like it. Just stop looking at me." Oh, the thoughts that tormented her when she was exhausted!

First, Lillian was lowered into the bathtub, though the smell of apple cider vinegar was so strong that she cried and clung to her grandmother. The miracle occurred when the fever dropped after the Unkers salve was applied to Lillian's neck and she had swallowed a dose of Infection Aid, a potent mixture of herbs.

Lillian was dressed in a clean flannel nightgown with an old cloth diaper tied around her neck, where the salve was already doing its work.

They pulled warm socks onto her feet, and she rested well, sleeping soundly for most of the forenoon as Mam busied herself doing the washing and then holding Benjamin.

Ruth suddenly remembered the box and brought it in, excitement in her eyes, a wide smile on her face. Her joy brought a tender look to Mam's own face as she remembered her daughter in easier times.

Slowly, Ruth lifted off the cardboard lid and found this box filled with groceries. Staples. Good, common sense pantry food. There was mayonnaise, ketchup, mustard—all expensive name brands.

"Oh, Mam! It's as if someone followed me around the bent and dent store and wrote down everything I couldn't find. Seriously. Coffee! Folgers. Just my favorite. I couldn't find it last time. Even pancake syrup! Mrs. Butterworth. Who is doing this, Mam?"

There were cans of navy beans and kidney beans, boxes of elbow macaroni and spaghetti, cake mixes and brown sugar, rice and flour and oatmeal.

"No name?"

"No clue."

Mam clucked her tongue and said she hoped the giver would be richly rewarded.

They used more of the ham that day, made bean soup with the broth, and ate large bowlfuls for lunch with grilled cheese sandwiches.

When Lillian woke, Mam said to try feeding her a bit of the bean soup, but she refused, turning her head from side to side, her lips squeezed tight. They opened a can of Campbell's chicken noodle soup instead, and Lillian ate spoonful after spoonful. She was extremely pleased with herself and all the praise they heaped on her, but she only smiled and promptly fell asleep before she could say a word.

When Mam's driver came late that evening, there was a mutual reaching for each other, a hug born of necessity. It expressed the great appreciation Ruth had for her mother and was absolutely essential for Mam to communicate her love and support for her daughter.

And so they stood, these two slight women, their coverings as white beacons of their subjection to God, and they drew strength from the warmth of human touch.

Ruth stood by the door and waved as Mam got in the car. Then she turned to go inside, knowing she would need to face the emptiness again.

Ruth's table had a round, brown placemat in the middle with a candle on it. As she headed back to her kitchen, she noticed a scrap of paper stuck beneath the placemat and tried to brush it away. Instead, she pulled out a check written to Ruth Miller in her mother's cursive hand, spaced perfectly as usual, and signed with her father's scrawl.

Again, Ruth got out her box of thank you cards and wrote her parents a note of heartfelt appreciation, grateful to know this time who to thank for the blessing. Then she put a stamp on it and hurried to the mailbox without a coat, her skirts flapping as she ran.

The air was invigorating, bringing color to her cheeks as she thrust the card into the mailbox and flipped up the red flag. She shivered and turned to race back to the house before she noticed a builder's truck bearing down, then slowing to a stop.

"Hello again."

She looked into John Beiler's eyes and smiled. Maybe it was the air nipping about her. Perhaps it was the fact that she was alone, the children already asleep in the house, or perhaps it was just the wonder of having to—no, wanting to—smile back at him, completely without guilt or wondering what anyone would say. No one would need to know. Not Mam or Dat or Mamie Stoltzfus.

"So you have a habit of going to the mailbox without a coat in the evening?"

"I'm afraid so."

He laughed then, and she continued smiling until the driver waved and John Beiler said, "Take care," as the truck moved off.

So. He was a builder. A carpenter, a contractor,

or maybe a roofer or framer or mason. There were so many different occupations that all fell under the general term of builder.

He was not a farmer. More and more, the Amish were moving away from farming since they were simply unable to complete with the huge dairy operations. However, many people Ruth knew still made a good living milking cows.

She had so enjoyed her life on the farm and still missed the satisfying "ka-chug, ka-chug" of the clean stainless steel milkers hanging from the cows' udders as they filled with creamy milk, the cash flow of the dairy farmers of Lancaster County.

Her main concern was Elmer and Roy. The boys needed chores—everyday repetitive responsibilities that build character—the way she was raised.

Times changed, and she needed to change with them. Still it troubled her the way Roy came home from school, sprawled on the recliner by the window, and read anything he could find, or fought with Barbara, or picked on Esther. He needed a job, more chores.

Well, there was nothing to do about that now.

When the boys came home from school the next day, their trousers and shoes were covered with mud. Elmer's hat was torn along the brim, and Roy sported a long, red scratch on one cheek.

"Football!" they announced when questioned.

"In the mud?" Ruth squeaked helplessly.

"It wasn't raining."

"Out! Out! To the *kesslehaus*. Get those pants off."

Laughing, with towels wrapped around their waists, they zoomed through the kitchen and down the hallway to their bedroom, soon reappearing in clean black trousers and white socks.

"That's better. Why did Teacher Lydia let you get so dirty? You shouldn't have played football in the mud," Ruth fussed as she picked up the mud-covered pants and placed them carefully in the wringer washer.

Roy eyed her quizzically. "Well, Mam, I'll just tell you one thing. You're not the teacher."

"Yeah, Mam. At least in school we're allowed to drag dirt into the classroom and no one yells at us."

Ruth eyed her growing boys and said they shouldn't have such a disrespectful attitude. They were not to talk like that to her. Boys enter a house with clean shoes or leave their shoes at the door, and if they couldn't respect their mother or her clean floors, then she guessed they should never get married. This statement was met with a great enthusiasm about how cool that would be. Girls weren't anything they cared about, and they were both going to be builders like John Beiler and never get married.

Ruth's head came up. "What do you know about John Beiler?"

"He is cool."

"He's awesome."

"Well…but…" Ruth hated the way she was stammering and hoped the boys wouldn't notice.

"He fixed the roof at school today. He was asking me and Roy all kinds of stuff."

"Yeah. He asked if we want to come help him lay stone along his flower beds."

"No, he didn't say flower beds. He said landscaping."

"What's the difference?"

"He said in the spring."

"Yeah. When it gets warmer."

Ruth stirred the bean soup and hid her face. She told the boys to get their chores done before supper. She was relieved when Lillian cried and she could turn her attention from all the confusing emotions the boys had stirred by talking about John Beiler fixing the schoolhouse roof.

Esther became Lillian's nurse as she recovered, spoiling her so thoroughly that she resorted to a babble of baby talk. The little nurse fixed a plastic tray of doll's dishes containing yogurt and chicken noodle soup and a few gummy bears, a small vase of plastic flowers, and a Kleenex folded in a triangle for a napkin.

Later, while Ruth washed dishes, Elmer stood beside her, snapping a dishcloth nervously and clearing his throat.

Ruth stopped washing dishes, looked into his eyes, and asked gently if there was something on his mind.

"No."

It was said much too quickly.

"Elmer, tell me."

He snapped the dishcloth, opened the silverware drawer, and closed it again. Then he said to the wall, "Mam, are you ever going to think about another dat for us?"

"Oh, Elmer." That was all she could say, his words having completely knocked the breath out of her.

"What does that mean, Mam?"

"It's just...."

"That if you did meet someone, he'd be stuck with all of us, too, right?"

Ruth knew Elmer had ventured into some turbulent, emotional waters. So she sat down at the kitchen table and asked him and Roy and Esther to join her.

"Elmer, I want you to know I would never, ever consider marrying again if that person did not want any of you. Besides, it's much too... soon. Your dat is still in my heart. He always will be. But he's not here now. You are. And you are a part of him, and the only thing I have to live for. I can never tell you how precious you are to me. The whole day I live to see you come home from school."

Roy's face shone with inner happiness.

"Boy, Mam!"

"You serious?"

"Of course I am. I don't have a husband, just you, and right now, you're all I need." Her smile was tremulous.

"But Mam, if you ever do want a husband, I think John Beiler's eyes look an awful lot like..." Elmer's voice dropped to a whisper as he finished saying, "my dat's." Then he put his head in his hands and the cried sweet, innocent tears of a young boy who missed his own father tremendously.

The next evening they decided to make Christmas lists, just for fun, pretending they had an unlimited supply of money.

Esther said she wanted a real playhouse—not the kind they could set up in the living room, but the kind they made at the shed place where Mamie's Ephraim worked.

"Oh my! That would be wonderful, wouldn't it? In the back yard, under the maple tree, by the row of pines. Okay, write it down. Let's pretend. What color, Esther?"

"White with black shutters."

"To match the house?"

Esther nodded happily.

"A porch!" Barbara announced.

"With a porch," Ruth wrote.

They wanted new scooters, a Gameboy, Monopoly, and all the books that Nancy's Notions had. Every single one. Elmer wanted bunk beds. Roy wanted a bow and arrow. Esther wanted a skateboard. And on and on until Benjamin started fussing, the clock struck eight, and it was time for their baths.

For their bedtime snack, they made popcorn and sprinkled it with sour cream and onion powder. They stirred chocolate syrup into their milk and discussed many silly subjects, along with some serious ones.

After Ruth had kissed the last soft cheek and collapsed on the recliner for a moment of rest before her shower, she realized she wanted a playhouse for the back yard so badly she could physically feel it.

Just as quickly, that dream's bubble burst, the pin named reality doing its job well. Ruth knew that a playhouse wasn't attainable and wouldn't be for a long time. That was okay. As Mam said, "*Siss yusht vie ma uf gebt* (That's just how things go)."

When the next box appeared on the front porch, the children squealed with excitement. Their enthusiasm turned quickly to disappointment when they opened it and found nothing inside except a small wooden box with a slot in the lid.

Elmer extracted an envelope from under the wooden box, tore it open hurriedly, unfolded the paper, and read, "Christmas wish lists. Please fold papers and insert in box. Put box on porch. Thank you!"

They gasped and lifted their round eyes to Ruth, questions flying as they reasoned among themselves. Who in the world? Well, they'd stay up all night. They needed a dog, that was what.

Ruth, who had returned to her quilting, smiled and burst out laughing after Roy devised a plan to trap the "box person," as they began to call him or her.

"I bet it's Mamie."

"They don't have extra money."

"Maybe they do."

"It's Helen."

"The driver?"

"No way."

Ruth looked up from her quilt binding and said they may never know, but they didn't really need to know. The giver would be blessed for his or her generosity, regardless.

She told the children to make new wish lists, but she asked them not to write down large expensive gifts. She did not want the person to feel obligated to fulfill every wish.

Esther gnawed her pen, glancing at her mother with cunning eyes, and then wrote in very small letters at the bottom of her list, "Real playhouse with porch. White with black shutters." She slipped it smartly into the slot cut in the top of the wooden box, right under Ruth's nose. After the children were in bed that night, Esther whispered to Barbara about what she had done.

Barbara was horrified at Esther's disobedience but said maybe it wasn't too serious, knowing Mam would love to have one, too. She had said so herself.

Chapter Eight

CHRISTMAS WAS FAST APPROACHING, AND the children marked each day with a large black X on the calendar, completely changing its appearance.

It was December thirteenth when they decided to hitch up Pete and go shopping together with the small amount of money they had. It was a Saturday, the sun was shining, and excitement hovered over the house as the children danced rather than walked, yelled rather than talked. Ruth barked orders, combed hair, and bundled everyone into clean coats and hats and scarves and bonnets.

They brushed Pete till he shone, cleaned the harness, hitched him to the buggy, and were off to the small town of Bart, which everyone called Georgetown. No one knew why Bart was the official address, since no one ever said Bart—just Georgetown—but that's how it was.

They were all snuggled into the clean buggy under the winter lap robes. Roy, Esther, and Barbara sat in back with Esther holding Lillian. Elmer sat in front beside Ruth as usual, holding Benjy.

Pete stepped out eagerly, and the buggy moved along smoothly around bends, past farms, up hills and down. They waved to oncoming teams, pulled to the side to allow cars and trucks to pass, and were very careful when they approached a narrow bridge. Ruth pulled firmly on the reins to allow a car to cross first.

As they approached the hitching rail at Fisher's Housewares, the row of parked horses and buggies left no room for them, so they drove past and pulled up to the fence beside it.

"You think it's okay to park here?" Ruth asked.

"Do you want me to ask someone?" Roy offered.

"No, we'll tell someone when we get inside."

The store was filled with so many things. The boys went off in one direction, and the girls in another, leaving Ruth with Benjy and a bit of time to buy some gifts for the children. It wasn't much, but it was all she could afford, and she wanted to be content.

The store was filled with others of Ruth's faith—some folks she knew, others she didn't. She tried hard not to be envious of the mothers with their carts piled high or a young couple discussing a purchase together.

Row after row of dress fabric, heavy pants material, bonnets, shawls, coats and sweaters, housewares, toys, beautiful sets of china, all sorts of kitchen wares, Christmas candy, books, and canning supplies—an ongoing display of every Amish family's needs.

Ruth chose a Monopoly game for the boys and a set of Melamine dishes for the older girls. Lillian would receive a small doll that boasted a 4.99 price tag. That was all she could afford this year.

She bought two serving dishes for her mam, two red handkerchiefs for her dat, a set of wooden spoons for Mamie, and some coating chocolate. She would make fudge and Rice Krispies treats.

Elmer and Roy begged for a set of books that was marked 29.99, and Ruth had to swallow the lump that formed in her throat. Oh, how she would have loved to buy them, wrap them in colorful Christmas wrap, and watch their faces on Christmas morning, the way it had been when Ben was alive—just last Christmas. But not this year.

Bravely, she handed her meager purchases to the clerk, smiled, and made small, cheerful talk, trying hard not to look around and want the items she could not have, the many things that were clearly out of her reach.

The children were quiet on the return trip,

sharing the small bag of Snickers bars wrapped in red and green wrappers. Ruth courageously told them that Christmas was all about the baby Jesus being born in the stable and not about worldly possessions or large gifts.

"Is that all we're getting, though?" they asked.

"Oh, no, your grandparents, your teacher, you'll get a lot more," Ruth assured them.

It was no wonder that Ruth cried that evening, the silent tears running unhindered down her cheeks as she allowed herself the luxury of letting her guard down for just one evening.

She found she could only be courageous for so long before her white flag of defeat went up. She allowed herself to roll around in self-pity and longing and all the stuff she was supposed to avoid but just couldn't help.

It was cleansing and solidifying to accept and admit that she was just one very lonely woman. She knew these were the times that eventually helped her to move on. This plain down honesty was refreshing.

She looked at her reflection in the mirror with her swollen eyes, the red blotches on her cheeks, and her scraggly hair, and she burst into a snort of hysteria before she moved out of the bathroom and away from the brutally honest mirror. Ruth reminded herself that God was still in His Heaven, so all was right with the world. She accepted her lot in life once more and was comforted by His presence.

Hadn't He provided a miracle in the form of that large sum of money that had appeared in a plain, white envelope in her mailbox and in the banana boxes and the generosity of her parents? Surely God was good, and here she was, whining and crying, ungrateful, and asking for more when she already had been given so much. Deeply ashamed, she knelt by her bed and asked the Lord to forgive her *undankbar* (unthankful) thoughts, remembering to thank him over and over for the Christmas miracles she had received.

Yes, He had chosen to take Ben, and yes, she was an *arme vitve* (poor widow), but even she could be caught unaware in the devil's own snares, the same as everyone else, perhaps even more so, if she tried to cloth herself in self-righteous robes of martyrdom.

Her spirit revived, her thoughts at peace, Ruth tucked her slim hands beneath her soft cheeks that had been cleansed by her tears, and drifted off to sleep. She slept like a baby, with Lillian creeping dangerously close to the edge of the bed as she tossed and mumbled her way across the expanse.

After her good cry and a solid night of sleep, Ruth enjoyed the Sunday day of rest with her children. On Monday morning, feeling refreshed, energetic, and more alive than she had for months, Ruth shivered on her way down to the basement to stoke the coal fire.

They had a good system. She shook the grate and watched the ashes for red coals, which were the signal to stop as all the cold, dead ashes had already fallen to the pan below. Then she pulled out the pan and slowly dumped it into a small metal bucket, where the few live coals would soon be extinguished in the pile of ashes.

Elmer and Roy took the ashes out and scattered them across the garden or beside the old tin shed. Then they filled the coal hod every evening and placed it by the stove, so she had coal in the morning to get the system going again.

She grunted a bit as she lifted the heavy hod of coal, watched carefully as the pieces slid into the hopper of the stove. She shut the lid, adjusted the thermostat at the side to three, and went back upstairs.

She had developed a habit of stopping by the back door every morning to peer through the window, checking the sky for the starlight—or blackness without them—that signaled a sunny day or a cloudy one.

She opened the door and stepped outside for a better view, peered into the early morning gloom, and found not one star. She could hear the traffic plainly, over on 896, so that meant the air was heavy, and rain or snow was just around the corner.

She missed the daily paper. Every morning, Ben had read the weather forecast to her as she stood by the stove frying eggs. Daily newspaper service was too expensive for her now, so she just checked the atmosphere and the stars before sorting clothes for a day's washing.

Not a nice wash day, she thought, but the boys wouldn't have enough pants to last until Friday, so she'd wash. She filled the stainless steel Lifetime coffeemaker half full of water, set it on the gas range, and flicked a knob to turn on the burner. She got down the large red container of Folgers coffee and spooned a portion into the top of the coffeemaker before quietly gathering hampers, dirty towels, wet washcloths.

She frowned as she entered the boys' room and stumbled on soiled clothes strewn across the floor, a sure sign of a significant lack of respect. How often had she asked them to please scoop up all their dirty clothes and throw them in the hamper? She'd even put a plastic laundry basket in their room—one without a lid—so it would only take one second to carry out this small act of obedience instead of two or three. Time for another pep talk.

Her hand slid along the top of the nightstand, searching for the small flashlight Elmer kept there. She grimaced when the alarm clock slid off the edge and crashed to the floor. Elmer lifted his head and blinked, his hair sticking up in all the wrong directions, a scary silhouette from the dim lamp in the hall.

"Sorry," Ruth whispered. "Getting your clothes."

He flopped onto his stomach, hunching his shoulders to pull up the covers, made a few smacking sounds with his mouth, and went back to sleep.

No flashlight. Well, she'd try and get everything although, inevitably, she always found a dirty sock or a crumpled t-shirt under the bed when she cleaned.

Now to start the diesel. No time or need for a sweater as she'd only be out for a minute. She stepped briskly out into the dark morning and took a few steps across the wooden porch floor before the toe of her sneaker connected with a solid object. With a startled cry, she pitched forward.

The old boxwoods by the porch softened her landing, crackling beneath her weight as she came to a stop. She rolled off the breaking shrubs, leapt to her feet, and brushed bits of mulch and leaves off her apron.

Ouch. Her shin was throbbing, painfully bruised from connecting with the edge of the porch, or…was it? Yes, it was another banana box. Well, she'd wait until the children awoke to let them experience the thrill of the box's contents.

When the first load of whites was being churned back and forth by the washer's agitator, the hot water and clothing rhythmically slapping the sides of the machine and the frothy suds appearing and disappearing, Ruth went to the kitchen, turned off the burner, and poured the boiling water over the coffee grounds. She set the top part of the coffeemaker over the emptied lower section and put it back on the stove to drip. The rich, flavorful aroma from the dripping coffee gave her a boost of energy and well being.

They'd likely have snow today. Wouldn't it be wonderful? Maybe they'd even have a white Christmas! The children could go sledding at Doddy Lapp's.

She went to the boys' room and whispered loudly, "Elmer! Roy! *Kommet* (Come)."

"Esther!"

Sleepy little sounds of denial met her voice, and she smiled, anticipating telling the children of her clumsy tumble into the bushes. Lifting her foot to a chair, she pushed down the black knee sock and examined the dark, angry bruise that had appeared there, surrounded by a faint bluish ring. She certainly had slammed that leg. Well, nothing to do about it now. Gingerly, she pulled the sock back up and went to feed the first load of clothes through the wringer.

After the water had been squeezed from the clothes, Ruth took up her hanging ring, a clever handmade item that was exactly that—a ring made of white PVC piping with wooden clothespins dangling from it, a few inches apart and attached by a sturdy nylon cord. All the socks, underwear, handkerchiefs, bibs, baby onesies, and numerous other small items were attached to the clothespins and, in the winter, carried to the basement to be hung above the coal stove, where they'd be dry in a jiffy. Those rings were a housewife's dream, and every wash day Ruth appreciated hers with her six children and all the piles of small, wet items to be hung up.

Back and forth she hurried with the Rubbermaid clothesbasket, up and down the basement stairs, making sure the boys and Esther were up and starting to pack their lunches.

It was an unspoken rule. If they heard the air motor and knew their mother was washing, they'd have to finish packing lunches for school. She set the brightly colored plastic lunchboxes side by side on the countertop each evening, put their pretzels in sandwich bags, and chocolate chip cookies, too. All they needed to do was make their own sandwiches and add an apple or canned peaches or pears.

Sometimes the children spoke wistfully about their classmates' food—the Gogurts with cartoon characters on the tubes or the Fruit Roll-Ups they wanted so badly that their mouths watered as they watched the other children eat. Their schoolmates sometimes had chicken nuggets or frozen pizza slices wrapped in tinfoil to put on top of the gas heater, and they smelled so good.

In response, Ruth had devised her own recipe for the children's lunches. She bought outdated packages of English muffins and spooned generous amounts of spaghetti sauce on top, using a jar of sauce she had canned herself. Then she laid a slice of white American cheese on top of each muffin. One day, Esther proudly told Ruth that Rosanna had wanted a taste of her pizza muffin, and now Rosanna's mother made them for her and her brother, Calvin.

Ruth poked her head through the kitchen

door. "There's ham salad, if you're tired of the pizza muffins."

"Nope!"

"Pizza!"

Smiling, Ruth carried the last load of laundry to the basement. When the clothes were hung, she placed the clothespin apron on its hook and rinsed the washer, hosing it down well with hot water. Then she got down on her hands and knees and wiped up any spilled water with a good, thick rag. There. Now let it snow. The laundry was all hung snugly in the basement, drying in the good heat radiating from the coal stove.

"Guess what?"

Roy was spooning spaghetti sauce onto three muffins, biting his tongue in concentration. Esther peered past his shoulder, disapproval written all over her face.

"Not so much!"

"Guess what?" Ruth said again.

"What?" Elmer asked, intently prying apart the slices of American cheese.

"Another box!"

"Nah-uh!"

"Serious?"

"Where?"

"Follow me!"

There in the cold, snow-laden air, they crouched, bending over the box with disbelieving eyes. There was another banana box, the same kind with Chiquita written in blue and yellow lettering and a picture of bananas. This one contained every item they had ever dreamed of putting in their lunchboxes. And some they hadn't even thought of—not knowing they existed.

"Jello already made!" Esther gloated, holding the small plastic containers high.

"Gogurt! Oh, I love these things!"

"Real candy bars!"

"Fruit snacks!"

"Crackers and popcorn and cheese curls."

"What's this?"

"String cheese."

"What's string cheese?"

There was ham from a real deli at a real grocery store and sweet bologna and a thick round of German ring bologna. The box was so heavy that Ruth took one side and Elmer the other so they could carry the box between them.

Quickly, she scrambled eggs for the children, hurriedly combed Esther's hair, and pinned her black apron around her tiny waist as she also goaded the boys along. "Brush your teeth!" she called over her shoulder as she hurried to her bedroom, responding to the morning sounds from Lillian and Benjamin.

Instead of opening the door the whole way, Ruth peeped through the small crack and said, "Peep!"

Mesmerized, Lillian sat straight up, watching the narrow opening. Up came Benjamin's head, his eyes wide with surprise.

"Peep!" Ruth said again.

Lillian bounced happily and then pitched herself onto her stomach, knowing Ruth would fling open the door and pounce on her, which was exactly what happened. Shrieking, she scrunched her little form into the farthest corner, and Ruth grabbed her warm, cuddly body and kissed her cheeks soundly.

"Morning, Lillian."

"Look, Benjy's awake!"

When Benjamin saw his mother approaching, he laid his head back on the crib sheet and kicked his little legs in anticipation. Lifting him, she inhaled his sweet baby smells and then carried them both out to the rocking chair for some cuddling, glad they had both slept through the washing.

As the school children went out the door, Ruth told them to be good and listen to the teacher. Their lunch boxes each held one of the containers of Jello. Ruth had told them they could only have one special treat each day. That way the food would last for a month, perhaps longer. They solemnly agreed, and Ruth was so proud of them.

Pride was something that wasn't named, since they were Amish. It was wrong to be proud of anything—one's home, husband, children, quilt-making abilities, baking skills, whatever.

So if Ruth was pleased, she didn't name it as pride. Compliments were often met with a shamefaced dip of the head or a word of denial. Even if true humility was actually in short supply, there was still an outward show of it.

Yes, this small ray of pride she would allow herself. She often felt inadequate and overwhelmed, raising these six children, so when the school aged ones readily agreed to make the treats for their lunchboxes last longer, she felt rewarded by their grave acceptance of her wishes. And she was proud of them.

Today, she would quilt. She would pin the new quilt top into the frame, the one her mother had given her when Ben died. It was a sturdy, wooden one with two rails resting on a stand at each end, allowing the quilt to be rolled as one side was completed.

She loved to quilt. It would be nice to have Mamie pop in to help her pin the back of the quilt to the fabric on the rails, but Ruth supposed she was still resting up from that hymn singing.

Ruth smiled. She loved Mamie. She was the epitome of every verse or poem ever written about friendship. Those words all held much more meaning since Ben had left her alone, to carry on raising the dear little ones on her own.

Not so little now, though. Elmer was turning into a miniature Ben with his shoulders held so high, his stance one of premature obligation as the man of the house.

And then, because the thought of Elmer's shoulders made her cry, her whole living room blurred and swam, and she couldn't see Mamie's form very clearly when her friend knocked on the storm door. Ruth thought it must be the UPS man and couldn't think what she had ordered that she'd be receiving a delivery.

When Barbara emerged from the girls' bedroom, rubbing the sleep from her eyes, she looked at the door and asked why no one let Mamie in.

Chapter Nine

"Hey!" Mamie decided enough was enough. That air was cold, and she let herself in through the back door into the kitchen.

"I'm here," Ruth called. "Just come in, you don't have to knock."

Mamie walked over, looked closely at Ruth, and said gruffly, "You were crying."

"Now, I wasn't."

"Yes, you were. I can tell."

And Ruth was wrapped in a compassionate embrace—never mind the odor of Mamie's sweater or the fact that her headscarf had once been white but now appeared gray and its fringes were hanging in Ruth's face. The love from her friend was the purest kind, bathed in glory.

"*Ach, siss net chide* (Oh, it isn't right), Ruth. *Komm*, Lillian. Come to Mamie. Hiya! *Vee bisht doo?* (How are you?)"

Sitting down, Mamie's motherly hands explored Lillian's head as she peppered her with caring questions, Lillian nodding or shaking her head no in response.

"Hiya, Benjy. You little corker! You're growing! *Ach*, Ruth, such beautiful children. Hiya, Barbara. Did you just get out of bed? Hey, I smell laundry soap. Don't tell me you washed already? If you did, I'm going straight home. Did you?"

When Ruth nodded, Mamie grinned shame-facedly.

"You know what? I'm fat and lazy. I have to go home and wash and go on a diet. But, oh my, it felt so good to roll over and sleep till seven. Eph has a dinner down at Stoltzfus Structures, so he said he'd eat Corn Flakes this morning. He's a wonder, that man."

She realized her mistake too late and clapped a hand across her mouth, her eyes widening in dismay.

"Ruth, I'm sorry. Here I go rambling on about my husband, and you having *zeit-lang* (loneliness and longing) for Ben. Don't listen to me."

"No, Mamie. It's okay. Don't worry about it. I'm happy that you love your husband. It's as it should be."

"Oh, Ruth. I wish I could....*Ach*, I don't know what I wish."

"How's Waynie?"

"Beside himself with his teething. I put that teething stuff on, but it hardly makes a difference."

Ruth nodded. There was a space of comfortable silence as they sat, Ruth pondering the significance of Mamie's earlier comment, and Mamie's eyes drifting to the coffeepot, nodding her head toward it.

Ruth put Benjamin in his high chair, made

toast and scrambled eggs, and filled a plate for Mamie. Mamie said she wasn't one bit hungry, but she managed to finish the last of the eggs as well as three slices of toast and two cups of coffee laden with sugar and milk.

She stayed, of course, to help pin the quilt to the frame, saying she simply had to go home as Fannie had a sore throat and Waynie might need her.

"Here, pull this over this way," Mamie said around the pins in her mouth.

"Is it crooked?" Ruth asked, realizing they'd have to unroll the whole backing of the quilt if it was.

"Stop pulling!"

"Which way?"

"My way!"

"I'm not pulling!"

"Yes, you are, too. Here, you go give Benjy some cereal or yogurt or something. Let me do this alone."

Ruth laughed out loud and said over her

shoulder, "Do it your way."

"You know what? You may be a much better *everything* than I am, but you aren't as good with quilts as I am. You can't pull on the backing. You have to roll it in naturally."

"Really?"

"Now you're *schputting* me!"

"No, I would never do that."

They both grinned, and Mamie took the pins out of her mouth and told Ruth she was closer to her than her own sister, that she was the best friend she ever had.

Ruth told her about the boxes that had been appearing on her porch, and Mamie's mouth started to wobble. Her blue eyes filled with tears, and she ran her hands across her large forearms and said it gave her chills.

"Who could it be? I'm afraid whoever it is doesn't realize how they're spoiling us," Ruth said, sitting down to spoon yogurt into Benjamin's mouth, which he opened eagerly, like a ravenous little bird.

"Who? Who would do something like that? Maybe a group of people. Maybe English people. Like a Sunday school class or something."

"Don't they go to Haiti or Africa or places like that? They have mission fields. You know—serious, big projects. Why would they bother with us? They don't know I'm a widow."

"Maybe they do."

"I don't like the word 'widow.' It sounds so lonesome, or sad…or something."

"I agree, Ruth, but that is what you are now. And before we know it, it will be a year. That's the proper time for remarriage, you know. I think you need to be reminded of that. Or do you?"

Never in her most intimate thoughts had it occurred to Ruth that Mamie would ever suggest the unspeakable. Her face flaming, completely at loss, she knocked over the container of yogurt, and it plunked solidly to the floor, splashing the thick, creamy mess all over the linoleum.

Leaving Benjamin in his high chair, she went to the pantry, grabbed the Cheerios box, and shook a few onto his tray. She kept her face hidden from Mamie as she got a clean rag from the drawer and proceeded to wipe up the yogurt without saying a word.

Wisely, Mamie busied herself with the quilt until Ruth had composed herself. Then she looked up.

"Well?"

"Well, what?"

"You know what I mean."

"I don't."

"You do."

"Alright, if I do, then who? Mamie, now come on. In all of Lancaster County there is not one man who would be....Well, think, Mamie, think about it—six. I have six children. A five-month-old baby. It's just too soon to speak of these things. And who would want all seven of us."

"Well, it's not too early."

Ruth looked up quickly.

"You are one determined lady."

"I sure am."

Then Mamie added, "You need a dog. If Trixie were here, you wouldn't have had to clean up that yogurt. She would have lapped it right up."

"All I need is a dog in this house, Mamie."

"If you had one, you'd know who is setting those boxes on your porch."

Ruth laughed.

"There. Now help me with this batting."

The soft, white middle part of the quilt was spread evenly across the rolled up backing. Then the actual quilt was tugged neatly across the top and pinned securely.

An appliquéd Rose of Sharon pattern in deep purple and shades of green was a sight to behold, they both agreed. The intricacy of the needlework was mind boggling, and the person who appliquéd was far more talented than the quilter, they confirmed.

"Oh, I just have to quilt a few stitches before I go," Mamie said longingly.

"You can stay."

"I have to wash."

Ruth knew, inevitably, that Fannie would do the washing, but that was none of her concern.

"I have a bit of a secret."

Mamie spoke as she was threading her needle, so she wouldn't have to look directly at Ruth. When Ruth was afraid to answer, Mamie went right on talking.

"Do you know who John Beiler is?"

"John Beiler?"

Ruth's voice was calm and quiet and so poorly disguised that she may has well have turned eagerly and pelted her friend with a thousand questions about him.

"You know who I mean."

Mamie drove her needle rapidly up and down through the quilt. She suddenly sat back and held up her thimble.

"This thing is too small. It pinches my finger."

"Here."

Ruth went to the sewing machine, located a larger thimble, and handed it to her friend.

"Yes, I know who he is," she admitted.

Seriously now, her face shining with concern and care, Mamie laid down the needle she was using and said, "Ruth, I saw at the singing, okay? I saw how he kept noticing you. And you were looking at him. Now, you need to know that he broke up with Paul King's Anna. They say it was him."

Ruth nodded weakly, the color leaving her face.

"Yes. They say it's awful hard on her. You know she's been a schoolteacher all these years. She's an attractive girl, gets along so well with the pupils, even the parents. I pity her. My heart just goes out to her."

"Yes," Ruth whispered, which was about the only sound she could manage.

"You know he's a brother to *Huvvel* Dave's Elam?"

Ruth nodded.

"Can't you talk?"

"Yes."

"Well, then act *chide* (right)."

They both burst out laughing, and Ruth cried a little. Mamie pushed back her chair and hugged her hard. She smelled of bread and butter pickles and Waynie's diaper, and when Mamie went home to do the washing, Ruth sat staring numbly out the window, her hands hanging limply at her sides. Barbara had to tell her two times that Lillian was in the candy drawer.

How can one lonely widow ever sort out her feelings? It was wrong to forget the memory of Ben, wrong to let another man into her life. Besides, what did Mamie know? No man—in his right mind—would consider her.

Ruth's emotions bounced back and forth for the remainder of the day between this new longing and her old loyalty. The emotions were coupled with the humiliating thought of putting herself through all these conflicting feelings when it was all probably just a crazy idea of Mamie's. Mamie was a bit of an airhead, anyway. But a compassionate, loving one at any rate, and she truly wanted what was best for her. Ruth knew Mamie was completely genuine—not even remotely capable of any cunning motives.

By the time the children came home from school, Ruth was an unstable wreck. She heated leftover spaghetti for supper and didn't answer their questions when they asked.

When the clouds settled low in the sky just before darkness blanketed the countryside and small flakes of snow started steadily falling through the cold, damp air, Ruth was surprised to see a truck pull in the drive.

That driver better get home, she thought. It looked like some serious hazardous road conditions would soon be developing. She turned back to the dishes, her mind elsewhere, and never gave the truck another thought since nobody ever came to the door.

Elmer and Roy burst back into the kitchen, their faces red with the cold, yelling at the top of their voices.

"Hey! It's snowing and *rissling* (sleeting)!"

"No school!" Esther cried.

Later that evening, Ruth read the story of Mrs. Boot, the farmer, at least three times. Lillian listened attentively, completely fascinated by the thought of the littlest pig being too small to get any breakfast and having to break into the hens' pen to eat theirs. After her youngest daughter had drifted off to sleep, Ruth tucked her carefully into bed before rocking Benjamin to sleep.

The boys studied their parts for the Christmas program, which was supposed to be a secret but hardly ever stayed that way. Then they yawned, took their showers, and dressed in clean sets of flannel pajamas. With their hair wet and faces shining from the soap and hot water, they each had a large serving of graham crackers and some milk.

Elmer said Roy had had to stay in for recess, but Ruth didn't hear what he said, so Roy kicked his brother under the table, hard. They went to bed, with Ruth answering them in quiet, absent-minded tones when they wished her a good night.

In the morning, her tired eyes showed that

sleep had evaded her. The fire was out, and she realized she'd forgotten to shake down the ashes and put more coal in the stove. The house was cold, but the darkness was alight with the white glow of the freshly fallen snow. Ruth did not bother opening the door to check the weather. It was too cold.

Making her way between the rows of dried laundry that hung from the line her dat had helped put up, she carried the ashes up the stairs, dumped them, and went to the tin shed to find a block of wood and a hatchet.

Setting the propane lantern on the floor of the shed, she brought down the hatchet, clunking into the piece of wood. She was rewarded by a splitting sound. Good. This would make perfect kindling.

"You want me to do that?"

In spite of herself, a scream rose to her throat, her hand went to her mouth, and she stared, horrified, at a dark form standing in the doorway. Clutching the hatchet, she straightened, without realizing what she was doing.

A low laugh was followed by, "Go ahead."

She looked down at the hatchet and then at John Beiler, who was also looking at it.

"Sorry. I really didn't mean to frighten you this way."

Finding her voice, Ruth asked weakly what he was doing here so early in the morning. She clutched her coat around her waist and realized she was still dressed in her ratty, flannel bathrobe, the one that had most of the buttons missing.

"I came over to put the key on the little hook by the playhouse door. I remembered last night after I got home."

"What playhouse?" Ruth did not understand.

"You didn't see the playhouse?"

"No. The…fire is out, and I hurried out here to chop kindling."

"Okay. Let's get the fire going. I'll show you later."

After a few masterful whacks, there was a pile of neat kindling that was then scooped up by the large capable hands that also picked up the lantern. He uttered a gruff, "Lead the way," and they were in the basement, where she found herself apologizing for the lines of dry clothes and wishing with all her heart she could take down the laundry ring suspended above the stove.

They said very little—at least not much that Ruth could later remember—till the fire crackled and burned. John added coal and then led the way up the stairs and out the back door. They crossed the newly fallen snow to the maple tree, where a small white playhouse with black shutters and a porch was set like a mirage. Ruth actually had to touch it before it appeared real.

"Oh, my word!" she said very softly. She was aware of him standing close behind her, and he bent his head and asked what she had said.

Softly she said, "But, who? I mean, why would someone put this playhouse here? How did it get here?"

Her hand traced the windows, the shutters, the posts that supported the porch roof, and she laughed, a happy response to receiving a gift and being glad of it.

"Do you like it?"

"Oh my!"

"Look inside."

She opened the unlocked door, and by the light of the lantern, she found a small room with a loft and a short ladder reaching up to it. The floor was covered with sturdy indoor-outdoor carpeting.

John followed her inside, and she held up the lantern, feeling very much like a child herself. The wonder of this perfect playhouse set in the clean, new snow provided the happiest moment of her life, at least since Ben had died.

"How soon can we wake the children?"

"We? Wake the children?" she asked dumbly.

"Can I? I mean, since I'm already here?"

She looked up at him, in the glow of the snow and the lantern light, and he looked down at her. And they smiled, a sort of shared conspiracy, as they thought of waking the warm, sleeping children and propelling them rudely out into the cold snow.

"Let's!" Ruth said.

"Should we let the boys sleep?" he asked.

"Oh no! They'll be excited just to watch Esther and Barbara."

"It is 6:30."

"Already?"

Everyone was rousted out of bed and bundled into coats and boots. Esther demanded an explanation, and Barbara yawned and sighed. Nothing could be worth getting out of bed before she was finished sleeping.

In the snow, they stood frozen, their faces broadcasting their disbelief—especially Esther, who appeared to be in shock.

"But, I didn't mean it," she stammered.

John put a hand on her shoulder, saying there was nothing to explain. Ruth was visibly puzzled.

They opened the door and examined every inch of the wonderful little house, climbing up the ladder, sitting in the loft, and becoming quite boisterous, the way children do when excitement runs high.

As the first light of dawn broke through the sky that was still spinning with snow, they all trudged back to the house. Ruth became flustered when Benjamin awoke, crying lustily from having been disturbed from a good night's sleep by the older children's chattering.

But John held out his arms, saying "*Komm.* May I hold you?" as naturally as if he'd had ten children of his own. Ruth handed Benjy over.

Benjamin sat sniffling but content, while Ruth got the children's breakfast on the table, lunches packed, and hair combed. All the while, she was miserably aware of the horrible old housecoat she was wearing and the fact that her hair was uncombed, her face unwashed. But it was a school morning, and there was a time limit.

John would not tell them who gave them the playhouse, in spite of repeated questioning, and only said it was snowing playhouses during the night. Elmer watched John, and they shared a man-to-man grin, one that made Ruth glad.

When the children left for school, Ruth put a hand to her hair and tried to salvage the scrap of pride she had left. John went down to the basement and put another hod of coal on the fire. When he came back up, he twisted his hat in his hands, cleared his throat, and asked if he could bring the children the rest of their gifts on Christmas Eve.

She said she supposed he could, but she had nothing for him.

"I don't need anything."

"Well, let me make supper for you then."

"That would be great."

"Would Saturday evening suit you?"

"Of course."

When he smiled at her, it completely banished the tortured thoughts in her mind. His eyes never left hers. There were long moments of shyness and kindness and understanding.

Would it be possible it could work? Before she lowered her eyes, she believed she knew the answer. It was up to him to lead her now.

Chapter Ten

MAMIE HAD A FIT. IT WAS THE ONLY WAY TO describe her gasping and hand throwing and head shaking and shrieks of glee.

"We're not dating."

"What else are you doing? Huh? Answer me."

"No, Mamie. You said he…they…I mean, they broke up only a few weeks ago."

"No, it was longer than that."

"How do you know?"

"I just do."

And so began an afternoon of cookbook searching, the likes of which Ruth had never seen.

Mamie kept insisting that the way to a man's heart was only accessible through his stomach.

They spoke seriously then of the near sleepless night Ruth had spent after Mamie had spoken to her about John Beiler.

"For me, Mamie, it was a sort of Gethsemane, a giving up of Ben. It was deeper than I ever realized. The letting go is so much more difficult that I thought. I cling to Ben, or rather to his memory, to get me through the days. I have to let that go now if I want to have another chance at…having a husband."

"So you have feeling for John?" Mamie asked, her hand stroking little Waynie's hair.

"Yes."

No hesitation, no pride, just a calm acceptance of something sent into her life that God had intended should be so. He knew when He would take Ben and knew when the time was right for John to be in her life, so there was nothing left but a spirit of willing acceptance, she told Mamie.

"But you're not dating."

"No. He's coming over for supper, that's all."

"Mmm-hm."

The turkey. It had to be turkey and stuffing, gravy, and mashed potatoes. Salad? Coleslaw? Red beet eggs?

Mamie made the best biscuits in Lancaster County, and her dinner rolls were perfection, but her whole wheat bread better than either of the two.

"Which one should I make?" she asked, never questioning whether or not Ruth wanted her to help.

"Dinner rolls."

"Men like biscuits."

"Do they?"

It was only Ruth's threats of never speaking to her again that kept Mamie from leaving a message on her sister Hannah's voicemail. They parted with the understanding that Mamie would promise to stay quiet about this.

"It's completely different, being a widow. Everything is top secret, and I can't trust you very well," Ruth had told her, which hurt Mamie's feelings a bit.

The secret didn't last long. Within just a few days, Mamie had told her mother, Hannah, and Ephraim, but they all promised to keep their mouth closed. Not a word. No sir.

Not until good-natured Ephraim *fa-schnopped* (gave away) himself down at Stoltzfus Structures. Before Saturday night even arrived, at least fifty people knew that John Beiler was having supper at Widow Ruth Miller's house. They all said they wouldn't tell a soul.

So, trusting and innocent, Ruth cleaned her house until it sparkled, polishing furniture, washing windows, moving from room to room, caring for the little ones in between scrubbing floors. That was on Friday.

On Saturday morning, she mixed the stuffing and put the turkey in the oven after packing it full of the fragrant mixture. Then she shredded cabbage across a hand held grater, mixed mayonnaise and sugar and vinegar, stirred it lightly, and scraped it all into a Tupperware container to chill in the refrigerator.

She cooked eggs for seventeen minutes, cooled them, and went to the basement for a jar of pickled red beets, one of applesauce, and one of raspberry preserves. She peeled potatoes, checked the turkey, watched the clock.

She made two pumpkin pies and one pecan, using her grandmother's recipe for both, hoping and praying they'd turn out okay.

She jiggled the pumpkin pies only a bit, to see if they were set in the middle, and breathed a sigh of relief when they stayed firm an hour later.

Elmer and Esther set the table, Roy folded napkins, and Barbara pushed Benjamin around in his walker. Lillian was the only problem, cranky and uncooperative all day, until Esther wisely observed her lack of motherly attention. The instant guilt provoked by her oldest daughter's attentiveness guided Ruth to her favorite rocking chair and the Mrs. Boot book.

The children were bathed and dressed, the

potatoes mashed and the gravy made, so Ruth left Benjamin in Elmer's care while she showered and dressed, choosing a deep plum colored dress, dark and demure enough for someone who'd lost her husband not quite nine months before.

She was grateful for the God-given gift of peace she possessed, somehow. The doubt and anxiety about the future was pushed aside, the darkness banished by the light of her new understanding. It was a gift, the best Christmas gift she had ever received.

She took a deep breath, though, to steady herself when the knock on the door did finally come.

"Do I look okay, Elmer? Roy, do I?"

"Perfect!"

"Yep. What he said!"

So with a smile on her face, partly a grin in response to her boys, she swung open the door and welcomed this kind man into her home.

His dark hair was neatly combed, his shirt a rich blue, his shoes clean and neat. If he was nervous, he did not show it, remaining relaxed and at ease with the boys.

It wasn't until they were ready to sit at the table that Ruth remembered the bread, or the lack of it. She said nothing, and when there was a knock on the back door, she wasn't a bit surprised. She knew her friend through and through.

Mamie entered without being told, her coat pinned over her ample stomach with two large safety pins, her grayish white headscarf tied beneath her plump face. Ephraim's camouflage hunting boots flopped on her feet, and she proudly bore a hot-cold bag from Walmart containing warm, crusty dinner rolls fresh from the oven.

"Thank you so much, Mamie."

She never heard or acknowledged Ruth but bent completely sideways in her strange attire and peered through the kitchen, searching desperately for a glimpse of John Beiler.

"I thought you were making biscuits," Ruth hissed.

Mamie was smiling, wiggling her fingers daintily at John. "Hiya, John."

"Hello, Mamie."

Mamie ducked her head shyly, then stepped back. "Men like dinner rolls," she whispered.

Ruth rolled her eyes, smiled, and said she'd talk to her later. But to her chagrin, Mamie stepped forward through the archway into the dining room, her safety pins prominent and gleaming silver on the black fabric of her coat. With a hand at either end of the scarf tied around her head, she jutted out her chin to tighten it and spoke very slowly and clearly.

"Well, John."

Oh please, Ruth thought frantically.

"So you bought the Petersheim place. Good for you. Now surely you know that house is much too big for one person to ramble about in all by himself. I mean, my goodness."

She tightened the scarf again, her face reddening a bit from the pressure, before resuming.

"Sorry to hear about you and Anna. But you know, sometimes things aren't meant to be, *gel* (right)? It's so nice to see you here at Ruth's table.

Well, I certainly hope you have a wonderful evening."

She wiggled her fingers at John, who thanked her and wished her a good evening in return.

The evening was ruined for Ruth. She'd never be able to look at John after that. Mamie let herself out, while Ruth busied herself doing absolutely nothing at Benjamin's high chair.

The turkey was browned and golden in the lamplight with the celery and onion stuffing sending up a rich, aromatic goodness. The gravy was creamy and full bodied, the chicken base giving it a golden color as it draped beautifully over the mounds of mashed potatoes.

The coleslaw was chilled to perfection with the shredded carrots making it colorful and the red beet eggs piled around it in a festive circle on Ruth's egg plate.

There was a moment of silence before John tried to put Ruth at ease saying, "You have done much more than was necessary."

Ruth found it too hard to meet his eyes.

"Ruth, don't worry about Mamie. I'm not embarrassed by her remarks. So please don't be."

It was only then that she looked up, met his understanding gaze, and felt the tension leave her body. She was comforted immensely. The remainder of the meal was a pleasure. John included the children in his easy banter, and they exchanged bits of news about the community.

Did they hear about the herd of cows that escaped their barnyard? It was the farmer's own forgetfulness as he was hauling manure and left the gate open.

Elmer was rapt, Roy completely taken. Esther ate her turkey and stuffing, her eyes shifting from one end of the table to John and then back to the other end where her mother sat, flushed and pretty. Barbara spilled her water and became so self-conscious that her eyes filled with tears. This did not go unnoticed by John, who jumped up quickly, snatched a tea towel from the countertop, and dabbed at the wet tablecloth while he teased her, saying she'd have to wash all the dishes.

He continued smiling at her, winning her over so completely that she forgot to eat as she was so busy watching his face.

Lillian ate a bit of turkey, pulled up her legs, and yanked off her socks. She sang her favorite song quietly to herself and thought nothing very unusual was happening. They simply had a guest for supper that evening. She was waiting for dessert. That was all.

When John saw the pecan pie, he told Ruth there was no way she could have known that was his favorite. When he tasted it, he sighed in appreciation and told her it was just like his mother's, and he wasn't kidding. He'd tried every restaurant in a twenty-mile radius, and none—not one—had pecan pie with that particular taste.

Ruth's eyes shone with gratitude. "It's likely the green-label Karo," she said.

He helped with the dishes, standing too close. What else could it be that made her throat constrict with emotion? She wanted to make a cup of tea and sit with him on the couch and tell him about Ben's death and the months that had followed. She wanted him to share her fear and worry and *zeit-lang* (loneliness and longing). She wanted to lay her head on his wide shoulder and feel the solidness of him.

Furiously, she scrubbed plates, berating her lack of control. These thoughts were shameful. Or were they? She was only human, wasn't she? Yes, she was only one lonely person with Ben's memory sliding slowly away, fading into the background, whether she was willing to admit it or not.

They played a lively game of Sorry, Roy's favorite. They made hot mint tea, and John ate his second slice of pecan pie, adding a dip of vanilla ice cream. Lillian ate two servings of ice cream, which Ruth doubted had been balanced by very many potatoes or vegetables. But for tonight, it was alright.

When it was an hour past the children's usual bedtime, Ruth announced the end of the evening, which was met with the usual whines and claims of unfairness. After a few minutes, they all accepted their mother's wishes, took turns brushing their teeth, and told John good night.

John looked at Ruth. "Should I leave now, and let you get your rest?"

No, John, don't go. Stay with me. Let this evening go on and on for all eternity. But what she said out loud was entirely different.

"That's up to you."

Looking at him, though, was her undoing. He held her eyes with his own, so dark and kind and compelling. I would love to stay, they said.

She smiled and asked if he would like another cup of tea or perhaps coffee. He smiled and said coffee would be great.

"Another slice of pecan pie?"

"I was hoping you'd ask."

She laughed and relaxed as they sat at the kitchen table. She helped herself to slice of pumpkin pie. He looked kindly at her and asked how she managed so well—all on her own.

She shook her head, a hand going to her throat.

"Oh, it's not the way it appears, believe me. I have my times."

"You would have to."

"I do."

"But you carry on so bravely. I…You know, I'll never forget when I met you that first time. I thought you must be babysitting your sister's children, or perhaps you had company and were taking your siblings to church…."

"Oh, come on now!" she broke in.

"I'm serious. You were…are so small, so young. I may as well be honest, Ruth. You look barely of age."

"What? I do, too!"

But she was smiling, a blush creeping into her cheeks, her lashes spreading against them as she lowered her eyes.

"Anyway, I asked plenty of questions, dug information out of anyone willing to answer. I was a real pest."

He grinned. He had a shadow along his chin, where the black stubble showed only a bit. My, he would be so handsome with a beard, the style required of an Amish husband.

"So when I found out the children were your own, I...."

She watched his face intently.

"I prayed. I asked God to show me the way. I truly meant every prayer. You see, I was dating Anna King, but...." He stopped, searching her face.

"Ruth, do you believe it's good to push two people together? When someone thinks two others would make a perfect match, so why not give it a try? I'm thirty-five, and everyone means well. They all want to help out. You know the way of thinking—poor guy, he just doesn't have the nerve to ask a nice girl out, so they try to play matchmaker."

Ruth laughed.

"So, I was dating, yes, but I think deep down I never really planned on marrying...her. Then, when I saw you...I saw Rebecca, all over again."

Ruth lifted questioning eyes.

"Once, long ago, I was in love, the kind of love that is rare. Completely head over heels. The romance book kind of heart throbbing love. And I thought, without a doubt, I would ask her to become my wife and live happily ever after.

"She was the type of girl who—let's say she had a roving eye. She kept flirting with other guys, but I would overlook it, thinking it was just Rebecca's way.

"I saw it coming—should have seen it long before I actually did. When she broke off the friendship, I vowed to never love again. I imagined myself the tragic martyr, the pitiful one, and for years, I thought wallowing in my lost love was sufficient. I didn't need a girlfriend, though Dat would have loved to marry me off."

He laughed, a rich baritone chuckle that brought joy to Ruth as well.

"So then I started my own roofing business. That became my life, my love, and…of course, God has blessed me, and I was able to buy the Petersheim place. I still feel God is richly blessing me far beyond anything I could ever deserve. It amazes me."

Ruth sipped her coffee but remained quiet. He smiled at her and told her she was a good listener, a rare quality in girls.

Ruth said she wasn't a girl. She was, at the age of thirty, practically a middle-aged woman—especially with her six children. And after having all them, she better know how to listen.

He laughed again, a repetition of his first joyous outbreak. And then he did something Ruth would never forget. Reaching across the table, he took her mug of coffee from her hand and set it carefully to the side before grasping both of her hands firmly in his own calloused ones. He questioned her with his eyes while maintaining a firm hold on her.

"Ruth you are an attractive and capable young woman, and I would love to know you better. If you believe it's possible that anyone else can take Ben's place, would you let me try?"

Her hands held in his strong, perfect ones, his

voice saying the perfect words. All the loneliness of the past months had been turned into a blessing. It amazes me, he'd said. Yes, it amazes me, too, John.

Arme vitve, weine nicht. Jesus will dich trosten. (Poor widow, do not cry. Jesus wants to comfort you.) Was this God's way of sending comfort? Or was she unchaste—thinking thoughts that were uncalled for before a year had gone by?

The simple clock on the wall ticked loudly. A drop of water escaped the confines of the faucet, followed by another, and still he held her hands, patiently watched her face, noted the conflicted emotions crossing the tender features.

"If…if you don't think it's too soon." She whispered the words, so great was her humility. He had to ask her to repeat them, leaning forward to hear the quiet words as she repeated them.

When he heard what she had said, he released her hands, and shook his head. "No Ruth. It's not too soon. We'll take it slow. The children need to have time to adjust. I'm very concerned about

Elmer and Roy."

Ruth nodded.

"Let me hear your story now."

"Would you be more comfortable in the living room?"

"We can sit there, of course."

So she told him of meeting Ben at age fifteen and never having any doubts. She told him about her marriage when she was nineteen, life on the farm, the devastation of his fall, the difficult times since then. All was spoken in her quiet, even tones, and as he listened, the ashes of Rebecca's love sprang to life, lit by the Master's hand, and he knew he would not have to journey alone any longer.

At the door, there was no awkwardness, no hesitation. He stood and held out his arms, and she stepped into them. His shoulders were as solid and as comforting as she had imagined, and she smiled against them.

It amazes me.

And he did not kiss her.

Chapter Eleven

JOHN PROMISED TO BRING THEIR GIFTS ON Christmas Eve, although they felt as if they'd already received so much. The teacher at school had given them pictures to hang on the walls of their rooms. The boys received a wildlife photograph, and Esther a beautiful poem with a yellow rose along the side. From Doddy Lapps, they'd received books and games and puzzles—far more than they'd thought possible.

And still the banana boxes appeared frequently and mysteriously in the night, sometimes dusted with powdery snow, but mostly just cold and always filled with useful items like fabric or towels, rugs, groceries, books, anything they could imagine. It became a ritual, the discovery of the banana box, a sort of race to see who would see the contents first.

Excitement ran high the day before Christmas. Their own meager presents were placed on the bureau in the living room, the absence of a tree so normal no one gave it a thought. A Christmas tree was unusual in any Amish home, so the bureau in the living room was the perfect place for the brightly wrapped gifts to bring cheer to the entire room.

It wasn't that Ruth didn't decorate at all. She pulled the box marked "Christmas decorations" out of the hall closet and distributed the red pillar candles around the house on windowsills and tabletops. She washed the plastic rings and placed them carefully around the candles.

A few snowmen were set beside the candles, and when the wicks were lit, the little snowmen seemed to come to life. There were no Santa Claus ornaments or any references to his coming down the chimney. Amish people had never believed in teaching children that myth, so there was no Santa Claus in sight.

The house was clean and bright, the cookies and candies set out on attractive trays. There was coffee, hot chocolate for the children, apple cider, seasoned pretzels, and popcorn balls.

Mamie, of course, had sent a huge platter of candy and cookies—so many, in fact, that Ruth considered not making any of her own.

She thought about inviting Ephraim and Mamie, but decided against it, afraid they simply wouldn't leave when it was time. Ruth smiled to herself as she set out the chocolate covered peanut butter crackers. She was ready to admit that she wanted time alone with John, and Ephraim and Mamie were notorious for staying up till four in the morning.

"Lillian, no!"

Ruth's words were sharp, bringing the busy three year old to a halt, halfway up the kitchen chair she'd pushed over to the bureau as she reached for the snowman by the burning candle.

Rushing over, Ruth grabbed Lillian around the middle, hauled her off the chair, and set her firmly on the floor.

"You may not have the candle. No, no."

"Candle so *shay* (pretty)!" Lillian protested.

"You just let it alone, okay? It will burn you, make an ouchy."

Lillian pouted and flounced off. She leaned against the couch, watching the flickering light on the little snowman.

There would be no supper that evening, they all agreed. Elmer did chores early, carefully sweeping the forebay in case John drove his horse and buggy. Esther said he didn't need to sweep as John would probably walk, but Roy asked how he would bring all the presents if he didn't bring his horse and buggy.

Elmer asked Ruth if she and John were…. His voice trailed off, and he lifted embarrassed eyes to his mother's face.

"Elmer, I was just waiting till you asked!" Quickly she slid an arm protectively around his shoulders, squeezing him affectionately, and looked into his eyes. "Do you wish I would not like John?"

Elmer shook his head.

"I won't think of doing this…I mean…well, Elmer, I hardly know how to say this. John did not ask me to marry him or anything. But if he did, and you would object, I would say no."

"I know you would." Elmer was very solemn, a mature soul in a child's form. His eyes searched Ruth's face intently.

"I would say no, Elmer. For you."

"But, Mam, if he does ask you, don't say no. We really need a dat."

"Does Roy think so, too?"

"Yeah. We talked about it a lot already. We think John Beiler is so much like we remember Dat."

"Really?"

So Ruth learned that her boys approved of John, which was a comfort. Esther just giggled and shrugged her shoulders when she was asked for an opinion, and Barbara said her mother needed help with the coal stove and removing the propane tank when it needed to be changed.

They all burst out laughing.

These dear children would always need to come first, Ruth thought. They may be facing another time of transition, but it would be made easier by generous amounts of explaining, understanding, and patience as she tried to ensure an atmosphere of stability in their young—and recently tumultuous—lives.

Yes, they approved, but she knew they would all have times of rebellion or disobedience. And yet her heart soared with newfound love.

The banana box came through the door first. There was no knock, no warning, just the door being pushed open by the cardboard box.

"Merry Christmas!"

"John!"

"Hey, are you the banana box guy?" Elmer burst out, unable to conceal his eagerness.

"You are!" Roy yelled, pointing his finger with a gleeful expression on his face.

"What are you talking about? I don't know a thing about banana boxes."

John took off his black coat, hung it on a hook in the laundry room, tucked his red shirt tail in his black trousers, and grinned.

"You left a banana box full of stuff on our porch. Every day almost!" Roy shouted.

"Shh!" Ruth was a bit embarrassed now.

"Why would I do that?" He caught Ruth's eye and winked broadly, and she knew.

Esther said she recognized his footprints in the snow, which actually made him pause and look questioningly at Ruth.

The boys were hopping up and down now, their brown hair flopping, their white socks like springs propelling them up and down, exultant in the knowledge of his discomfort.

"Gotcha! We gotcha!"

"It was you!"

"We know it was!"

"You have no way of finding out!" John said.

"Take off your shoe."

"We'll measure the tracks!"

"Tracks? What tracks? You can't do that. Tracks widen with the sun's heat. When snow melts, it changes the shape of the shoe's mark. Or suppose I wore my boots?"

Too late, he caught himself, then threw back his head and laughed uproariously. Elmer and Roy pounced on him and tried to make him sit down so they could remove his shoes.

It all ended with Elmer and Roy overpowering him, landing him on his back on the living room floor, where he laughed as Roy held him down and Elmer undid the laces of his black shoes. Happily, they raised them high in the air, then slipped out the door, standing in the snow in their stocking feet to carefully evaluate the length and width and pattern of the footprints. They burst into a gleeful cheer and gave each other a high five before rushing back into the house.

"Yup, they match. It was you!"

John conceded, and the children suddenly became shy, watching him with careful expressions.

"Was it really you?"

"Why did you do it?"

The questions flew thick and fast, till John put up a hand and said if they all hushed, he'd tell them about it.

"I saw you driving the horse to church at your Doddy Lapp's house and asked many, many questions afterward. I decided your mam could not have an easy life and no doubt could use some help. It was my pleasure. I have no children, you know."

"So, what about the playhouse?" Barbara asked.

"It snowed playhouses that night, I told you!"

"You're *schnitzing* (fibbing)!"

"Mamie's husband works at Stoltzfus Structures, remember?" Elmer watched John's face, saw the seriousness.

"He does, that's right. I bet it was Ephraims."

"It would be just like Mamie," Roy agreed.

Ruth met John's eyes and played along. She knew Eph and Mamie could not afford a new playhouse, but she'd let John trick them, for now.

What fun!

"Wow, I didn't know Eph had money."

"Well, you know how Mamie bakes. I bet she made five thousand dollars making Christmas cookies."

"Nah, Roy!"

"Hey, two thousand! Three!"

There was a discreet knock on the door, and Ruth's heart sank. Oh please don't let it be Ephraims. How could a person love a friend the way she loved Mamie and cringe at the thought of having her and her family there with John?

It wasn't right. As the Bible said—actually Jesus had said—it was wrong to give high seats to classy people, or those of high status, and barely acknowledge those of lower class.

Mamie was not lower class. She was just relaxed and dear to Ruth's heart. And Ruth knew she was only being selfish, desperate to have John to herself, so she flung open the door, letting in a blast of cold air and a tumble of children and Mamie and Ephraim and Trixie, the dog.

John looked surprised, then pleased. Ruth let out a quick sigh of relief. It was okay.

"Trixie! *Ach* my! Trixie!" Mamie raised embarrassed eyes to Ruth's face.

"Children! Fannie! Why did you bring Trixie? She wasn't supposed to come. Ruth, *fa-recht* (for real)!"

As usual, Mamie fussed and explained, taking coats, pushing children forward, as Eph stood smiling eagerly, saying nothing.

"Well, here we are, crashing your party. *Siss net chide, gel net* (It isn't right, is it)? But our noses grew steadily longer all day. I told Eph I can't stay at home. Trixie! Fannie, get Trixie. Put her in the *kesslehaus*. Waynie, no. Mam will smack your patty. Waynie!"

Moving with remarkable speed, she flung herself at her ambitious little boy, who was scuttling along, intent on the potted palm tree in the corner. She grabbed him by the waist band of his black Sunday pants, swung him to her shoulder, and patted his bottom a few times.

"Here, Eph. Take him."

Waving a hand to cool her reddening face, she scooted back to Ephraim who received little Waynie with a solid thunk, whereupon the small boy set up an awful howling.

Ruth watched and smiled, catching John's eye. Yes, the evening would be extremely interesting.

John and Ephraim got along fine, of course. Mamie whispered to Ruth that everyone liked Eph. He didn't know what it would be like to meet someone and not have them like him.

Then she spied the presents, and said, oh my, you didn't have your gifts yet? Ruth assured her it was alright. They would exchange gifts in spite of them being there.

So Mamie settled herself on the sofa, eager anticipation shining from her generous blue eyes. Trixie repeatedly yapped from the *kesslehaus*, very effectively driving Ruth to distraction.

The children were seated now, on the floor or on chairs. Esther clasped her hands in her lap—dutiful and restrained like a much older child.

Barbara was trying hard not to bounce up and down, but she kicked one foot constantly. Lillian squirmed and wiggled and bounced and squealed. She clapped her hands and tried to lift the lid off the cardboard boxes, until her mother sternly told her to sit down and hold still for a minute.

Elmer was very grown up, holding Benjamin, trying to hide the excitement he must be feeling. Meanwhile, Roy let his spill out all over the place, bouncing and hopping from one end of the living room to the other.

"Now your children don't have anything," Ruth told Mamie quietly.

"Oh, they will in the morning. They know that."

First Ruth gave the boys their package. Eagerly, they tore off the inexpensive wrapping paper, crumpled it, and held up the new Monopoly game, exulting in the game they knew they would play with every single evening.

Barbara and Esther were equally pleased to receive the set of dishes, explaining to Mamie's girls that their dishes were either lost or broken, and this was exactly what they wanted.

Lillian gazed in disbelief at the doll in the box, the wrapping paper in shreds at her feet. "*An dolly* (A doll)." She could only whisper the words, so great was her delight. Mamie watched her tenderly and had to put a hand to her eyes to hide the ever-present tears of love that lay just below the surface.

John watched quietly. Then he got up and slowly lifted the lids of the boxes he had brought in, extracting one neatly wrapped package with a huge red bow on top. Ruth saw the bow and stored it away mentally, knowing it would adorn the gift that she would give to her parents on Second Christmas.

For the Amish, the day after Christmas is called *Ztvett Grishtdag* (Second Christmas). It is merely a continuation of Christmas Day, allowing for additional gatherings and festivities with the typically large extended families. Ruth looked forward to the time with her parents and siblings.

These days of Christmas always meant large meals, plentiful and generous gifts, afternoons of singing Christmas songs, and eating lots of snacks and delicious pastries. There was homemade candy, cookies, and trays of fruit, and the children playing endlessly with their cousins as the tempo of the day was fueled by their sheer exuberance along with a good dose of sugar.

"Elmer!" John said and smiled as he beckoned the boy to him.

Shyly, blinking self-consciously, Elmer went to receive his gift, muttering a quiet, "*Denke* (Thank you)," before returning to his seat, where he held onto it, unsure of what to do.

"*Machs uf!* (Open it!)"

Mamie gave him clear orders but then felt she was being bossy, if only for a second, Ruth could tell. Elmer looked at Ruth, waiting for her approval. She nodded her head.

It was unbelievable! Ruth could tell by his numb expression that the contents of the box extended far beyond his belief. An entire set of

bird books and real binoculars! What a gift! Elmer
couldn't say a word. He just picked up the binoculars and turned them over and over in his hand,
tracing his finger over the sturdy field glasses before lifting them to his eyes.

Eph said he'd be up to borrow them right before hunting season, then slapped his knee and
laughed very loudly, bringing a smile to John's
face. Ruth thought he would, likely.

When John called Roy's name, the boy cata-
pulted from his seat, scooped up the large box, and
plunked it on the floor, already ripping the green
and red wrapping paper from it. His eyes bulged,
and he yelled. He yelled and yelled and yelled. He
didn't stop even when he held up a large, heavy
skateboard and dove back into the box to retrieve
a set of knee and elbow pads in the same brilliant
blue and darkest black hues as the skateboard.

Ruth shook her head at John and mouthed,
"Too expensive." She was rewarded by a look so
generous it took her breath away.

Esther's box contained the exact same thing,

except hers was pink and black. Very, very pink—more like florescent magenta! She looked straight at John and said as maturely as possible, "Thank you, John. It's exactly what I wanted."

It was only later, in the privacy of her room, that she threw the skateboard on the bed, flung the knee and elbow pads on top, raised her arms high, and did a sort of tap dance, all by herself, where no one could see. She was just thrilled.

Barbara didn't have a package, so she thought, until John told her to wait a minute and went outside. He returned with a little wooden table and two benches. He told her to wait again while he went back out and brought in two chairs, one for each end.

Barbara smiled behind both hands. Then she sat down on the bench, patting the space beside her. John doubled up his tall frame and sat very carefully on the small space she allowed him. They both tilted their heads to one side and smiled very grown up smiles at each other.

It was as if John could not help himself, then,

and he reached out an arm and squeezed her affectionately. She settled an elbow on his leg and kept it there while Mamie blinked furiously, her mouth working as she clamped a hand across it to keep her emotions in check.

Lillian had a large package wrapped in children's giftwrap with Winnie-the-Pooh all over it, dressed in Christmas reds and greens. The box held a child's vacuum, a broom, mop, and dustpan, a small ironing board, and a highchair for her doll. Very solemnly, she pulled each thing from the box, piece by piece, then stood up straight as a flagpole and asked where her iron was.

John became a bit flustered, but he got down on his knees and poked around in the box, finally coming up with an iron to go with the ironing board, relief clearly written on his face.

Lillian took it, examined it carefully, and said, "Thank you, John." She set up the ironing board and plopped it on top. She ironed for the remainder of the evening, pausing only when Waynie got in her way.

Finally John brought Ruth a brilliant sparkly gift, the light catching the silver glints in the red wrapping.

"It's heavy!" she gasped.

"Is it?"

Mamie hovered over Ruth, a protective friend and a very nosy one, John did not fail to see. He watched as the small hands carefully lifted the wrap beneath the scotch tape and folded it neatly away, repurposing it in her mind along with the bow.

When she opened the box, a small gasp of surprise escaped Ruth's lips, and her eyes filled with tears. Mamie's piercing shriek carried across the room, slammed into the walls, and ricocheted back to John's ears.

"Ruth!"

"Oh my!"

"Mam!"

"It's what you wanted!"

There it lay—the rubbed luster of the cherry wood an oval of perfection, the glass so clear and clean, the face so golden and white. It was a Swiss rhythm clock, nestled in white tissue paper with the batteries tucked in at the bottom. A clock is a traditional Amish engagement gift, but that didn't even cross Ruth's mind. All she could think to say at the moment was a simple, breathless "*Denke*."

They carefully lifted it out of its box, inserted the batteries, and huddled around with bated breath, watching in wonder as the small castle below the face turned back and forth.

When the hands reached the eight and the twelve, the soft strains of "Amazing Grace" pealed from the beautiful clock, and Ruth lifted her face to John's, touched his arm with her fingertips, and told him it was the most wonderful gift anyone had ever given her. And she meant it.

Was it because she was older, more spiritually aware? Or was it the surprising joy of a second chance when she had felt so alone? Whatever it was, the wonder of this beautiful timepiece infused her Christmas season with the magic that is only carried by a truly grateful heart.

Chapter Twelve

CHRISTMAS EVE LASTED ON ONTO CHRIST-
mas Day, as Ruth knew it would. Ephraim and
Mamie and the children settled themselves in,
delighted by this opportunity to become better
acquainted with John.

They made hot chocolate with Mamie's recipe.
When she found out Ruth had no Reddi-whip,
Mamie put on her coat and scarf and marched the
whole way home for some of her own, saying hot
chocolate was not the same without it.

John declined the sweet drink. After all that
bother, Mamie fussed at him, but he smiled and

said he was a black coffee drinker, if that was okay. He certainly did not want to offend her. She said fine, drink what you like, but she was noticeably quieter than usual for the next half hour until Ruth made a big fuss about her hot chocolate recipe, which set things right.

They played Monopoly with the boys' new game. They ate candy and cookies, fruit, and Chex Mix and popcorn, until the house appeared to have been stuck by a hurricane.

Ruth winced as Waynie sat on the floor with a small chocolate bar melting in one little hand and a wedge of Rice Krispies treat in another. He was soon on his hands and knees, crawling across a braided rug that wasn't washable and leaving a trail of sugary stickiness in his wake. Meanwhile, Mamie waved her hands and exulted in her acquisition of Indiana Avenue, having finally acquired a set of three, her messy little son the last thing on her mind.

This was not lost on John, who watched Ruth watching Waynie, and knew she truly was an exceptional person.

Ephraim easily won the Monopoly game as Mamie dropped out early after spending all her money to put hotels on her properties. Unfortunately for her, no one landed on them, so she never collected any rent. She soothed her battered ego with the taco dip and tortilla chips, then made another batch of popcorn, and ate almost the whole bowlful by herself.

The children played and played. They laughed and shrieked and ran around the house until midnight, when even Esther began to yawn, and they all had to go to bed. A large air mattress was set up on the living room floor, and two children were tucked in on the couch with soft, clean sheets for each one. Soon Ephraim's children were nestled down for the remainder of their stay.

Weariness was creeping stealthily over Ruth by two o'clock, and John saw the shadows under her eyes and the heaviness of her eyelids. He stretched and yawned, saying it was way past his bedtime and he was going to call it a night.

Ephraim asked what in the world was wrong with him. The night was still young, and what was the use sleeping—that was all a waste of time. Mamie laughed hysterically at her husband and said she agreed. She was up for another game of Monopoly.

John stayed adamant, however, and Ruth told him how grateful she was as they washed dishes.

He stuffed wrapping paper in garbage bags, swept, and picked up toys for Ruth to put away. They hung the new clock on a large nail on the wall above the sofa, then stood back to admire it. It said 3:10.

"It's almost morning!" Ruth exclaimed.

"It's Christmas Day!"

"Merry Christmas!"

"Merry Christmas, Ruth."

And then, because he wanted to take her in his arms so badly, John decided to leave, and he did so rather hurriedly, leaving her with a great sense of loss and bewilderment. Ephraim and Mamie took their leave as well, prodding the older children awake for the walk home and picking up the sleeping little ones.

What had gone wrong? Why had John left so quickly, when she yearned for his arms to hold her close, embracing her in their safety and solidness? He had said nothing at all about seeing her again.

Miserably, she brushed her teeth, weariness seeping into her bones until she collapsed into bed and cried exhausted tears of disappointment.

It was Mamie. Ruth bet anything he didn't like her and her rowdy family. They shouldn't have come. But she was only being Mamie, her dear friend, her loyal supporter, and Ruth knew she could not desert her. If John wanted to be that way, then so be it.

Everyone slept till 8:30, when Benjamin's little grunts first woke her. Ruth rolled over, opened one eye, and found Benjy's eyes peering intently at her through the bars of his crib. Immediately, she was filled with good humor and called his name in soft tones. He lowered his head and kicked his legs and squirmed with happiness, then propped himself up on his hands and watched her again.

She got out of bed, scooped him up, and nestled him in the bed beside her. She held her baby close as she breathed in the smell of him, that mixture of Downy fabric softener and Johnson's baby shampoo and formula and pacifier. She tiptoed down the hallway to the living room to rock him in the recliner for a while.

The light was grayish white. It was snowing! On Christmas Day! She stood in her nightgown, holding Benjamin, and marveled at the clean beauty of the falling snow.

"*Schna*e! (Snow)!" she told Benjy. He smiled, his eyes alight, and reached for the new wonder in his life, so she took him out to the porch and let him touch it, delighting in the amazement in his eyes.

They had sausage gravy and homemade biscuits for breakfast with dippy eggs and toasted bread, leftover fruit, and cereal.

Lillian said her doll was named Goat, and when everyone made fun of her, she threw a terrible fit, kicking against the bench and screaming so loudly that Ruth had to take her away from the table. She returned to scold the children in firm tones, telling them Lillian was only three, and if she wanted to name her new doll Goat, she guessed they'd get used to it. Then she burst out laughing in spite of herself with all the children joining in, while poor Lillian lay on the couch and sniffled.

Well, it was Christmas, but with six children, these things happened, and no mistake about it. For a mother, it was called life—no matter what day of the year.

She was bewildered when Mamie tapped on the door, her wide face shining with exhilaration, excitement, and what else?

"Merry Christmas, Ruth!"

"Well, Mamie! What are you doing here?"

"You could wish me a nice Christmas," she said, and Ruth promptly did.

"Thanks," Mamie sniffed her indignation before announcing that she was babysitting.

"Who are you babysitting?"

"Your children."

"But why?"

"Here." Reaching into her coat pocket, Mamie brought out a sealed, white envelope with Ruth's name on it.

Completely puzzled, Ruth opened it and unfolded a plain sheet of paper. She read the words in Mamie's handwriting, but they made no sense. Please walk to this address. 11749 Gravel Road. Thank you.

Ruth looked up. "But why? Where on Gravel Road? Is it far? It's snowing."

"Oh, just go. No, it's not far. Dress warmly."

"What is going on, Mamie?"

Mamie was divesting herself of her coat, undoing the large silver safety pins as she spoke, the children watching, strangely quiet. The boys didn't ask to see the contents of the letter, which was strange. Esther and Barbara were setting their dishes on the table without any show of curiosity.

"I know. It's Ephraim. He's playing a trick on me."

"No, he'd never do that on Christmas Day. He's still in bed, sound asleep. You know how lazy he is on holidays."

And some other days, Ruth thought, but said nothing. She combed her hair hurriedly without bothering to wet it down or roll it tightly—just ran a comb through it and shrugged into her dress and apron, warm socks and boots. She donned her heavy, black coat and white headscarf and pulled on her gloves, but she couldn't conceal her bewilderment.

Mamie had settled herself in the recliner with Benjamin on her lap, showing him a small animal book and looking as clueless as the boys.

"Don't you care that I'm venturing out in this cold snow, perhaps putting my life in danger?" she asked Mamie, who looked up at her with guileless blue eyes and didn't as much as crack a smile.

Was it just her imagination then or did she actually see the boys and Mamie peering out from the front window, glee plastered all over their faces? What was going on?

The snow was gorgeous, though, and her spirit responded to the clean stillness of it as she reveled in the hushed whisper of the falling snow. She loved how it clung to fencepost tops and tree branches. It was piling up on roofs and mailboxes and bushes, changing the drab landscape into a clean, white wonderland.

God was amazing, the way He designed each new season with the brilliance of newly fallen snow a great boost to late fall's frozen drabness.

11749. Where in the world? Oh. There was the Petersheim place. She'd have to check the mailbox. What if there was no number on it? She looked to the left, then right, standing still at the end of Hoosier Road, indecisive.

He stood inside, peering anxiously through the windows, the trees in the front yard a filament of snowy lace obscuring his view. All morning, he'd been pacing, watching. Would she come?

11749 was the Petersheim place, but the fact that John had bought it and now lived there somehow eluded Ruth on that snowy morning.

It must have been the minimal amount of sleep. Five hours of it, to be exact.

She walked along the winding driveway. It was on level ground with great trees on either side, and beyond them the whispering snow fell, creating a scene from some other world, a fictional land.

The house had two stories with a porch along the front. There was stone of brown and gray, low windows and a massive front door, alcoves, dark beige siding, and roofs of various levels.

It couldn't be the Petersheim place. It looked like an English house, almost. Oh my.

Ruth had never actually been at the house before. Her church district stopped at the end of Hoosier Road, so a neighboring district had their church services there.

There was a large barn, a shop, a stone sidewalk that had been swept clear of snow. There were pine trees and bird feeders alive with colorful winter birds. Brilliant red cardinals vied for position with bold blue jays, and anxious little black-capped chickadees twittered about, while the wily nuthatches climbed down tree trunks headfirst.

The shrubs were numerous, trimmed with a shelf of snow. Oh, what a beautiful home. Hesitant now, her steps slowed. Carefully, she placed one foot on the stone sidewalk and looked at the house.

The front door moved, opening from inside. John Beiler stood in the doorway and welcomed her to his home. Blank, her mind not comprehending, she stopped.

"But…"

His heart pounded now, afraid.

"Come in. You must be cold."

"No."

"Aren't you?"

"No. I just don't understand."

She stopped by the front door and pulled off her boots, one gloved hand going to the stone wall to steady herself. John told her to bring them into the house, and she set them carefully on the rug inside the door before looking up into his face. He was so pale, so obviously ill at ease.

"Why did you ask me to come to here? It was you, wasn't it? What did Mamie have to do with this? What's going on?"

Ruth looked so bewildered, so at a loss. John was so terribly unsure of himself, too. He knew he couldn't wait until he'd shown her around the house to say what he had planned, so he left caution behind and put his hands on her shoulders, which were still wet from the snow.

"I'm nervous, Ruth. I....oh, come here."

He pulled her into his arms, lifted her face after a few moments, looked deeply into her eyes, and slowly lowered his head. She closed her eyes as his lips met hers, hesitantly, afraid somehow, but her love spoke to him, and he kissed her with a new and wonderful love of his own.

"Ruth. Ruth."

It was all he could say.

Tears streamed down her face, cleansing her of the months of grief and loneliness, the doubts and fears, the fires of widowhood, the times when she thought she could not go on for one more day.

When he realized she was crying, John was concerned, afraid he'd done everything all wrong.

"I'm sorry. I shouldn't have. Ruth, please."

Clumsily, he handed her his red handkerchief, and she unfolded it to wipe her eyes and blow her nose, telling him she must look awful.

"But why are you crying?"

"I guess because I'm here, and you just kissed me, and it's been so long, and being alone with six children is so hard sometimes. And because I love you so much."

He drew in his breath.

"I'm sorry, John. I just do. I know you're supposed to say that first, but…"

"I love you, Ruth."

"As I love you."

Then he took both her hands and held them together against his chest and said, "Will you marry me, Ruth?"

"Yes, I will. But not till April."

"I figured." And he kissed her again with a newfound possessiveness, and she felt her whole world tilt and right itself, the stars in her eyes and heart a harbinger of things to come.

"Do the children know?"

"Oh, yes. And Mamie."

"Which means Ephraim and Hannah and whoever else she could get ahold of."

They laughed together, then, warm and comfortable, as easily as if they had known each other forever.

He took her hand and led her throughout the house. As they moved from room to room, she realized how incredible it really was. The upstairs was still empty, but she noted that the children could have their own rooms now. And there was a guest room and two—no, three—bathrooms. The kitchen was far too beautiful, and she told John so. He replied that she deserved everything, all of it. They would buy bunk beds for Elmer as Roy would still want to share a room with his brother.

Ruth suddenly stopped. She looked at John

and asked if they would always remember to place their trust in God in such a place. She was afraid she'd forget to do that, living here with him.

"I mean, John, that isn't…*ach*, how can I say it? For months, I've had to trust God to help me daily. With things like the coal fire in the basement, the propane tanks—everything Ben always took care of, and now I cannot *begreif* (comprehend) the safety and security of living here with you."

She slipped her small, soft hand into his large, strong one, and he held it as carefully and as reverently as he knew how as they stood in silence. Some things just had to stay in the heart until the right time, he decided. He had a whole lifetime ahead of him to speak of his love and to distribute it over the years, enriching their marriage repeatedly and building that love into a satisfying union that eclipsed all expectations.

The snow fell around them, the pine tree branches bending with the weight of it, as they stood hand in hand on Christmas Day. Ruth's heart was full with the richness of the many sudden and unexpected blessings in her life—ones that she would never be able to take for granted following the lonely and difficult months she had endured. She knew her days as an *arme vitve* would enrich her life with John far above anything of earthly value.

The End

The Glossary

Arme vitve — A Pennsylvania Dutch dialect phrase meaning "poor widow."

Begreif — A Pennsylvania Dutch dialect word meaning "comprehend."

Chide — A Pennsylvania Dutch dialect word meaning "right."

Dat — A Pennsylvania Dutch dialect word used to address or refer to one's father.

Denke — A Pennsylvania Dutch dialect word meaning "thank you."

Dienna's frau — A Pennsylvania Dutch dialect phrase meaning "minister's wife."

Do net — A Pennsylvania Dutch dialect phrase meaning "don't."

Doddy — A Pennsylvania Dutch dialect word used to address or refer to one's grandfather.

Fa-recht — A Pennsylvania Dutch dialect word meaning "for real."

Fasht dag — A Pennsylvania Dutch dialect phrase meaning "fast day." October eleventh is the day most Amish people set aside as a day of fasting and prayer in order to prepare themselves for the fall communion services. Another fast day takes place in the spring on Good Friday.

Fa-schnopped — A Pennsylvania Dutch dialect word meaning "gave away" as in "revealed."

Gay — A Pennsylvania Dutch dialect word meaning "go."

Gel — A Pennsylvania Dutch dialect word meaning "right."

Gooka-mol — A Pennsylvania Dutch dialect word meaning "let me see."

G'mya — A Pennsylvania Dutch dialect word meaning "g'morning."

Huvvel—A Pennsylvania Dutch dialect word meaning "planer" or "grater." It can be used to designate someone who works with these tools.

Ich gleich dich so arich—A Pennsylvania Dutch dialect phrase meaning "I love you so much."

Kaevly—A Pennsylvania Dutch dialect word meaning "basket."

Komm—A Pennsylvania Dutch dialect word meaning "come."

Kesslehaus—A Pennsylvania Dutch dialect word meaning "wash house."

Luscht Gartlein—A devotional book used by the Amish that can be translated as "Lust Garden" or "Love Garden" because it encourages the development of a spiritual lusting or longing after God.

Machs uf—A Pennsylvania Dutch dialect phrase meaning "open it."

Mam—A Pennsylvania Dutch dialect word used to address or refer to one's mother.

Mommy—A Pennsylvania Dutch dialect word used to address or refer to one's grandmother.

Of age—One is considered "of age" at 21 years old.

Ordnung—The Amish community's agreed-upon rules for living based on their understanding of the Bible, particularly the New Testament. The *ordnung* varies from community to community, often reflecting leaders' preferences, local customs, and traditional practices.

Rissling—A Pennsylvania Dutch dialect word meaning "sleeting."

Rumspringa—A Pennsylvania Dutch dialect word meaning "running around." It refers to the time in a person's life between age sixteen and marriage. It involves structured social activities in groups, as well as dating, and usually takes place on the weekends.

Sark — A Pennsylvania Dutch dialect word meaning "care for."

Sark feltich — A Pennsylvania Dutch dialect phrase meaning "caring."

Schnae — A Pennsylvania Dutch dialect word meaning "snow."

Schnitzing — A Pennsylvania Dutch dialect word meaning "fibbing."

Schputting — A Pennsylvania Dutch dialect word meaning "mocking."

Schtruvvels — A Pennsylvania Dutch dialect word meaning "stray hairs."

Sei — A Pennsylvania Dutch dialect word meaning "his." In communities where many people have the same first and last names, it is customary for the husband's name to be added to that of his wife so it is clear who is being referred to.

Shay—A Pennsylvania Dutch dialect word meaning "pretty."

Siss net chide—A Pennsylvania Dutch dialect phrase meaning "it isn't right."

Sits ana—A Pennsylvania Dutch dialect phrase meaning "sit down."

Undankbar—A Pennsylvania Dutch dialect word meaning "unthankful."

Unfashtendich—A Pennsylvania Dutch dialect word meaning "senseless."

Vee bisht doo—A Pennsylvania Dutch dialect phrase meaning "how are you?"

Zeit-lang—A Pennsylvania Dutch dialect word meaning "loneliness and longing."

Ztvett Grishtdag—A Pennsylvania Dutch dialect phrase meaning "Second Christmas." This is the day after Christmas when many Amish people continue their holiday celebrations with their large, extended families.

More Books by Linda Byler

Available from your favorite bookstore or online retailer.

"Author Linda Byler is Amish, which sets this book apart both in the rich details of Amish life and in the lack of melodrama over disappointments and tragedies. Byler's writing will leave readers eager for the next book in the series."
—*Publishers Weekly* review of *Wild Horses*

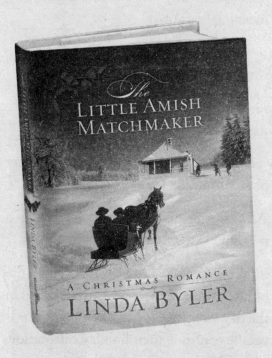

THE LITTLE AMISH MATCHMAKER
A Christmas Romance

About the Author

Linda Byler was raised in an Amish family and is an active member of the Amish church today. Growing up, Linda loved to read and write. In fact, she still does. Linda is well-known within the Amish community as a columnist for a weekly Amish newspaper. She writes all her novels by hand in notebooks.

Linda is the author of six series of novels, all set among the Amish communities of North America: Lizzie Searches for Love, Sadie's Montana, Lancaster Burning, Hester's Hunt for Home, The Dakota Series, and the Buggy Spoke Series for younger readers. Linda has also written five Christmas romances set among the Amish: *Mary's Christmas Goodbye*, *The Christmas Visitor*, *The Little Amish Matchmaker*, *Becky Meets Her Match*, *A Dog for Christmas*, and *A Horse for Elsie*. Linda has co-authored *Lizzie's Amish Cookbook: Favorite Recipes from Three Generations of Amish Cooks!*

LIZZIE SEARCHES FOR LOVE SERIES

BOOK ONE

BOOK TWO

BOOK THREE

TRILOGY

COOKBOOK

SADIE'S MONTANA SERIES

BOOK ONE

BOOK TWO

BOOK THREE

TRILOGY

LANCASTER BURNING SERIES

BOOK ONE

BOOK TWO

BOOK THREE